# Pirats

A Tale of Mutiny on the High Seas

*Rat Tales, Part Two*

By Rhian Waller

Printed in the UK

First Printing, 2018

ISBN 978-0-244-38650-4

Cover image by @Tofu_Soup

Inside illustrations by Gill Thomas

Maps drawn by Rhian Waller with reference to the
Mercator map.

*With thanks to Anna, Ato, 'Rat' Dave, James, Jenny,
Kaitlyn, Mark, Michelle, Nadia, Sheila and my mother
for helping me plot and steer the course of this
adventure.*

*To Barrie for feeding me and our ratties and showing us
all the patience and affection we need.*

*Finally, to the ratties themselves. Without you, Leeloo,
Priss and Ripley, these books would not exist. Just stop
chewing holes in my rough drafts!*

# Characters

**Rip:** The main character. Older sister to Lu and Preen. She is a very ordinary brown rat and does not trust humans. She does not like fighting but will do battle when necessary.

**Lu**: A daft white rat. She is friendly and clumsy.

**Preen:** The third rat sister. Grey, pretty and shy.

**Pew:** Skip of the rats. He is old and creaky but leads with cunning and wisdom.

**Patch:** A young orphaned Pirat. He has a marking over one eye. He is cheeky and likes to play.

**Peg**: Brother to Patch. He is missing half a leg but this does not slow him down. Also cheeky.

**Spite**: A rat who comes aboard from a slave ship. She has seen the worst of humanity and it has left her with a fear of rules. She wants to have no master. She has a big gang which includes **Stink**, **Sharp** and **Twitch**.

**Gold**: A handsome blond rat from the slave ship. He takes a liking to Rip.

## Bigs

**Runa**: A Swedish girl who is on her way home from Jamaica. She has bonded with **Lu** the rat.

**Abel**: Cabin boy on the *Liberté*. He appears to have lost the power of speech. He is terrified of rats.

**Blanche Fleur:** A Haitian woman dressed in white. She is rescued from a sinking ship. She has a talent for navigation.

**Rouge Fleur:** The woman in red, also rescued. She is not a sister of Blanche: the women are so close they choose to share a last name.

**The Captain:** A Dutch man who is in charge of the *Hydromyst*, at least for now...

# Sections

# Author's Note

Welcome to the second book in the *Rat Tales Trilogy*, dear reader!

As in the first book, *Ship Rats*, these events are rewritten from the notes of an eminent naturalist who had the opportunity to spend time with these rodents in the late 18th Century.

For those who have just joined us, these are the adventures of Lu, Rip and Preen, three rat sisters, and a Swedish stowaway.

During their voyage to Jamaica, the three young rats had to undertake a series of challenges set by Black Spot, the terrifying Skipper of the rats. Through a mixture of cunning and bravery, they managed to survive these dangerous tasks, but Black Spot was not about to let them stay aboard.

He was furious that Lu made friends with a Big girl (rats call us 'Bigs' because of our gigantic size). A great storm struck the *Hydromyst*, their ship. Lu had to use all her wits to escape Black Spot and save the ship. They arrived safely in Jamaica, but the story did not end there…

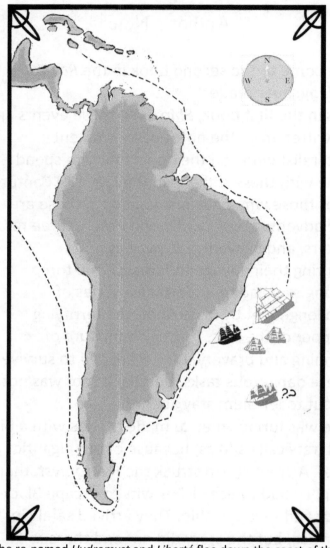

The re-named *Hydromyst* and *Liberté* flee down the coast of the New World.

# Chapter 1: Going home?

Lu was missing.

Rip crouched at the fore of the ship. Her nose twitched. She could smell salt, fish and clean air. Her whiskers told her something was going to happen. Every man aboard was busy, loading crates or checking that the craft was shipshape. They were docked at the port of Golunda in the warm Caribbean islands and now it was time to sail.

Rip was a rat. She was only three months old but she was larger than little Lu and their sister, shy Preen.

Lu had explored the port town but Rip stayed aboard. She worried that her sister would be left behind on land.

The brown rat scurried along the handrail and looked out over the dock. She sniffed as hard as she could. Yes, there was Lu. Rip still couldn't see her.

'Hurry up, Lu,' she said.

The little white rat was snoozing in a special purse bought just for her. This purse hung from the shoulder of a young girl, Runa, who was eleven. Runa argued with the tall man walking her to the gangplank. Rip sat and listened, though the words meant nothing to her.

'I don't want to go,' said the girl. 'I want to stay here with you, Pappa.'

'Runa, I love you very much and soon I will be home but until then you must continue with your schooling. I would be far happier if I knew you were safe in our house with your friend Astrid rather than here.' Runa's

Pappa waved back at the town, which was full of rum and rambunctious sailors. 'I will send word you are to have a new teacher.'

'Can I learn the natural sciences, about animals and things?' said Runa.

'No, Runa,' her father laughed. 'You will learn needlework and deportment. And of course you will continue with your French and German.'

Runa pushed her chin out and her lips went thin.

'Pappa, I –'

'Don't turn our farewell into an argument,' said Pappa, and then he used his special name for her. 'Little love, we can talk about this when I come home. I know you are not an ordinary child, my daughter. An ordinary child would not have tried to post herself to Jamaica in a box, or made friends with a white rat. Go home Runa and perhaps when I return we will find you a tutor who can teach you these things.'

Then he kissed her on the cheek and she hugged him hard, careful not to squish her rat purse.

'Thank you Pappa,' said Runa. Then she ran up the gangplank and turned to wave.

Rip did not come too close. She was not a fan of humans – which she thought of as *Bigs.* Even Runa, who was not all that huge, was a great, giant clomping thing to a ship rat.

Rip could not understand why Lu liked the company of Bigs, but then Lu had always been silly.

Rip trailed Runa, who walked across the deck to her cabin. The brown rat dashed through the door and shot under the bed. Preen was waiting there. The grey rat had an excellent instinct for finding food and she knew Runa was good at giving out treats.

'Hi Rip!' said Preen.

'Lu is back. She is up there with the Big.'

'Oh, that's good,' said Preen. 'I'm glad.' She paused to wash her face.

Runa tipped the purse up and Rip heard a little *plop* as Lu fell onto the mattress. Rip pushed her claws into the bedframe and climbed up.

'Lu!' she said, hopping across the lumpy mattress.

'Oh, Rip,' said Lu, blinking sleepily. 'Hi.'

They sniffed nose-to-nose, which is the rat way of shaking hands.

Rip jumped when Runa sat beside them.

'Well ratties,' said the girl. 'It seems I am to become a lady. I'm not sure I want to learn how to recite poetry and sew. Are you two hungry? Wait there and I will fetch you a good breakfast.'

Lu and Preen pranced about, hoping for food. Rip stayed dignified.

'Here we go!' boomed Runa as she returned from a hamper with an armful of snacks. 'I brought plenty for all of us. Help yourselves. Make the most of it, we'll be back to salt meat and biscuit soon enough.'

She cut up the vegetables and fruit with a little knife and laid the slices on the bed. Preen soon had bits of banana on her whiskers but Rip hung back.

'Eat, Rip,' said Lu.

'No,' said Rip. 'I don't trust Bigs. I don't need a Big to find me food.'

Runa noticed Rip backing away. She squatted down and offered her a scrap of meat.

'Here you go, brown ratty,' said Runa.

Rip accepted the gift and nibbled it watchfully, but when Runa pushed a finger to rub the rat's nose, Rip dropped what she was chewing and nipped the girl's hand. At the same time, she squeaked: 'No.'

It wasn't a hard bite. It didn't break the skin, but Runa still gasped.

'Ow!'

Preen and Rip scattered at the sound. Lu followed.

'Don't hurt my Big,' said Lu. Rip felt bad.

'I can't let her touch me,' she said. 'I don't like it, but how can I tell her to stop? Bigs don't speak. They just make that long, loud noise that hurts my ears.'

'Well I want to eat more food,' said Lu, and she returned to the feast.

Preen nibbled her fur nervously, but whatever she was going to say was lost when both rats felt a shudder run through the ship.

'We are on the move,' said Rip.

Sure enough, the *Hydromyst* made its way toward the open sea. Soon, it turned and started making headway toward the rising sun.

Rip heard the familiar sounds of creaking wood and waves, but it didn't comfort her. She was in disgrace. She wandered off alone, down to the deck that the rats used as a playground and meeting place. The sailors used this space to store rope so it wasn't as busy as other parts of the ship.

Pew, the skipper of the rats, sat in a nest he'd made among the ropes.

He was old and smelly, but everyone liked him being in charge because he didn't boss them around or steal their food like the last Skip. He was wily, and other rats came to him for advice.

'Yarr, Rip,' he said. 'How are ye?'

They sniff-sniffed a hello.

'I bit a Big,' said Rip. 'Now I feel bad.'

'Who cares?' said Pew. 'A Big is a Big.'

'I don't care about the bite, but now I think Lu and Preen are cross with me.'

Pew sneezed.

'Go be a ship rat,' he said. 'Eat good food, run and play, have fun. Time will heal this.'

'Yes,' said Rip. 'You're right.'

The truth was, Rip was happy the ship set sail. Lu enjoyed exploring Jamaica, sniffing the fragrant flowers, digging in soil and chasing the chickens while Preen spent a lot of time remembering Mum Rat and pining for home. But something about the salty sea breeze and the motion of the waves felt right to Rip. She enjoyed being on the ocean. Once she got home, she might miss being on a ship.

She made her way to the front of the *Hydromyst*, bouncing up the stairs and scrabbling on to the stem that jutted out over the waves. She sat like a little brown figurehead, enjoying her own company and watching the horizon rise and fall. At sundown, the Bosun brought her a snack of ship's biscuit and a lick of stew in a bowl. He thought the rats were good luck.

'I don't need Bigs,' Rip told herself, 'but I will eat this.'

The *Hydromyst* was well away from the island when dusk fell. Rip liked the twilight, but to her the world was a blur of blue. Her nose was sharper. The breeze brought her a strange new smell from another ship. It set her fur on edge. It was a blend of sailing scents – wood, canvas, tar and rope, but it was mixed in with sweat, fear and human muck. Rip shivered. Whatever this new ship carried, Rip wanted to be far, far away from it.

A few moments later the wind blew from another direction and Rip tasted clean air. The strange, frightening ship sailed away into the night.

# Chapter 2: Save Our Souls

The next morning, they came across another ship. This time, the sailors got very excited. Rip was hiding in the cargo hold. She still hadn't apologised to Lu or Runa.

'Rip? Rip?' a rat called. It was her friend, Sleek. 'Where are you?'

Rip dropped to the ground and scampered out of the cabin. The deck was a forest of legs and the air was full of shouts.

'They are in distress,' said the first mate. 'Ready the jollyboat.'

The Bosun and Captain were at the handrail on the port side of the ship, swapping an eyeglass back and forth. Rip crept over to a scupper, a gap in the side of the boats. This was where deck water drained off. It made a perfect window for a curious rat. She smelled other Bigs, lots of them, men and women. Her nose sensed excitement, gunpowder and metal.

'It's a barque. There are ladies on board,' said the First Mate. 'I can make out their skirts. They are waving hankies.'

'Yes,' said the gallant Captain. 'We must attempt a rescue. Bring the ship around and launch the jollyboat when we are close.'

'Aye sir.'

'Can you see what is amiss?' said the Captain.

'She's low in the water, sir,' said the First Mate. 'She could be wallowing.'

Rip stayed hidden as the sailors trimmed the sails, bringing the *Hydromyst* closer to the stricken vessel. The new ship was smaller. Rip looked down on the deck where a dozen Bigs shouted, waved and beckoned.

'Oh, oh,' she heard one of the Big women wail. 'Help us good sirs!'

She spoke in French, which was as meaningless to Rip as the Dutch spoken on the *Hydromyst*, but the Captain, who was a cultured man, understood.

He cupped his hands around his mouth to shout back, deafening poor Rip.

'Keep calm. We are launching a small boat to ferry you to us. Where is your skipper?'

The woman was slight and had powder on her face and chest. Her hair was done up in neat curls beneath a wide hat and she wore a fine white frock. Rats have no interest in clothes, but Rip thought the long skirts and ruffles would make a good hiding place. She hid her face in a gloved hand. The other held an umbrella.

'Alas, our good captain went overboard along with many of the crew,' the woman in red mourned. Though she leaned on a walking stick, she smelled young and healthy to Rip. 'There are thirty souls on board.'

Rip heard the jollyboat land with a splash. Four sailors strained at the oars. Still, the *Hydromyst* edged nearer. Rip didn't like how close they had come to the sinking ship.

The woman in white allowed a sailor to help her down a ladder and into the boat. The woman dressed in red found a seat. She still clutched her stick. Oars plish-plashed as they scooped through the water.

'Thank you,' said the tearful woman in white as the sailors of the *Hydromyst* helped her aboard. She swooned. The first mate went to comfort her.

The jollyboat ferried over twice more. Turning to the woman in red, who clung to his arm, the Captain asked, 'How many are there?'

'Enough,' she said. She let go of his arm and grabbed her stick, pulling it in half. There was a click, a scrape, and suddenly the Captain had a blade at his throat. The woman in white, meanwhile, recovered from her fainting fit and pulled the cloth from her parasol. A sharp tip glinted as it pressed against the first mate's belly. Now that they were close, it was clear her skin was far darker than the makeup that covered it.

'Cannon ready!' the woman in white shouted loudly enough for her voice to carry over the water.

Rip heard a clatter of wood and a rumble as the shutters on the port side of the barque flew open. Iron muzzles appeared in the square frames.

'Pirates!' shouted the Bosun, but it was far too late. The sailors of the Hydromyst had expected a rescue, not an attack. One had the sense to ring the deck bell until a pirate pulled out a flintlock pistol and pointed it at him.

Some of the sailors had swords, though, and they surrounded the newcomers. Others swarmed up from the lower decks, armed with anything they could find. The cook carried a cleaver.

'Release the Captain,' said the Bosun.

'Not a chance,' said the woman in red. She spat on the deck. 'Throw down your weapons.'

'You're outnumbered,' said the Captain. His Adam's apple bobbed against the blade.

'And you're outgunned,' said his captor. 'You ain't got a cannon, not a single one. We'll blow this fat pig of a ship to splinters.'

'With you on board, ladies?'

'Aye, with us aboard,' said the woman in white.

'You seem like a reasonable gent,' said the red woman. 'But we ain't ladies and we ain't reasonable.'

There was a long moment where all Rip could hear was the wind, the waves and the sound of dozens of human hearts beating too fast. She made herself small. This wasn't the way rats did it, but she recognised a fight when she saw one.

'Stand down, men,' the Captain said at last. 'We're merchantmen, not fighters.'

'Good choice,' said the woman in red. 'Drop 'em.'

Rip flinched as steel hit the floor.

'Abel, be a dove and pick up the gents' razors, butterknives and marlinspikes,' said the woman in white.

A small Big started to put the improvised weapons in a sack. He smelled nervous.

Just as Rip was wondering if she should make a dash for the cabin and find her friends, a new scent came to her. She sniff-snuffed deeply. There were strange rats!

A blur of movement caught her eye. Something small dropped from the woman in white's shoulder. A brown shape swaggered over to Rip. She instantly forgot all about the Bigs and their strange drama.

It was a young buck. He had light brown fur with a darker blotch over one eye.

'Nice to be on our new ship,' he said.

'Who's this?' said a second rat. He moved with a limp. One of his legs was a stump, but he was quick despite the missing paw.

'A girl!' said the first rat. His whiskers danced.

Rip was not impressed.

'Get out of my face.'

'That's rude,' said the stumpy rat.

'You can't be rude to us on our own ship,' said the eye patch rat.

'This is not your ship!' said Rip.

'It is now,' said the stumpy rat. 'We took it.'

Rip bristled.

'Oooh, oooh, she wants to fight us!' said the eye patch rat.

Rip forced herself to settle down. She willed her fur flat. She'd only fought once before and it hadn't been fun. She didn't like the hollow feeling of rage and how it left her shaky afterwards. She remembered fur flying and teeth flashing and gnashing. She did not want to do it again, no matter how cheeky these young rats were.

The strangers puffed themselves up. They danced, walking sideways with stiff legs. This was a sign they planned to attack.

Meanwhile, the Bigs were having their own row.

The two women had stretched a rope across the deck.

'Alright, sailor-boys,' said the one in white. 'My name is Blanche Fleur. My good friend in red is Rouge Fleur. We offer you a choice.'

'That side, you end up in the brig and we put you off at the first port we land in. Step this side and join us. We don't want our nice new deck messed up with blood.'

'Don't step over the line,' the Captain roared. 'This ship needs at least fifteen men to crew it. They won't be able to run both ships by themselves.'

'That won't bother us,' said Blanche. 'If no one crosses the line we'll just put a hole in the hull and let you sink.'

She gestured to the cannons gaping from the gun deck.

Two men stepped over the line. Rip recognised them as sailors who had caused a lot of trouble on the way to Jamaica. One was a drunken sailor, the other used to be the Second Mate before he was demoted.

'Good men,' said the pirate lady. Slowly, two other sailors crossed over, then another and then two more. The Captain was left with his First Mate, the Bosun and a handful of loyal men. Not one of them budged an inch. The Captain folded his arms and looked stern.

'Lock 'em up,' said Rouge. Two of the pirates bound the loyal sailors' hands.

'Traitors,' said the Bosun.

'I'm sorry, Skipper,' said one of the free sailors, shamefaced. 'I have a girlfriend in every port. What'll they do if I get offed by a pirate?'

'I'll take you, you, you and you over to my ship,' said Blanche, pointing to the newly recruited pirates. 'Five of my best men will stay here, with Rouge as your captain.'

'A woman?' whispered one of the *Hydromyst* sailors. He was quiet, but not quiet enough. A burly pirate slapped him across the ear.

'Not a woman, a *captain*,' said Blanche.

The crew split, with varying amounts of regret. The red lady, meanwhile, set her own men to task.

'Search the ship,' said Blanche. 'Someone pick up the rats.'

One of the pirates looked around.

Rip and the two boy rats were still sizing each other up. She was bigger, but there were two of them and one of her.

She puffed up her fur. Their fluffed theirs out too.

She turned sideways and stood on her tip-toes. They did the same.

A thin hiss slid from between Rip's teeth like the sound of escaping steam.

This was a stalemate.

All three of them froze as two leather boots slammed down on each side of the trio.

'Which ones, Ma'am?' the Big pirate said.

'All of them!' Blanche shouted.

'Aye.'

Suddenly, Rip found herself in the dark. She was caught in a cloth prison. She squeaked and struggled as the walls pinched together, squishing her up to the two strange rats.

'What's this? What's this?!' Rip raged. Paws pressed into her side. She could feel her tail kink up. Her nose poked into a soft belly. The world lurched and everything turned over and opened out. She saw sky again. The pirate had scooped her up in a tricorn hat and was carrying the three rats across the deck.

'I will bite you,' Rip shouted. 'I will!'

The Big didn't understand or care.

'Calm down,' said the rat with three legs. He seemed quite relaxed as the pirate climbed one-handed down a cargo net and into the jollyboat. The pirate flexed his muscles and started to row to the new ship. The waves rocked them up and down.

'Put me back, Big!' Rip squeaked. Her wedge-shaped head looked in every direction but she couldn't see an escape route.

The pirate had placed his hat on one of the seat-planks. He rowed hard. The only others in the boat were the woman in red and the small Big who smelled of fear. The little Big sat as far from the hat full of rats as the small boat would allow.

'Don't be afraid of them,' said Blanche.

The boy nodded but said nothing.

'Yo ho and home we go,' said one of the strange rats.

Rip, though, had never felt so far from home.

## Chapter 3: Aboard the *Liberté*

The new ship was a confusion of sights and smells. The sharp tang of chemicals and the blunt, bloody smell of iron were everywhere. The vessel was overloaded with cannons.

The hat full of rats was lifted up and passed into a waiting pair of hands. Rip felt helpless as she peered over the rim. She looked into a Big's face. It was the woman in red. Her nose and eyes filled the world. Her breath flattened Rip's fur.

'You picked up three for the price of two here,' she laughed. 'I have an extra rat!'

She reached out. Rip saw the approaching fingers come into focus.

'NO!' she said. 'Don't touch me. Don't!'

The finger snapped back.

'She's a bit of a madam, boys,' said the Big to the two other rats who wrinkled their noses as they listened. 'I hope you get on with each other.'

The pirate lady tipped the hat out and Rip landed with all four paws on the deck. As soon as she touched solid wood, she dashed away. The other rats followed.

'Hey, grump rat,' said the one with a missing leg. 'Slow down.'

Rip did not slow down. She was cross, she was scared and she did not like this strange new place.

She shot across the deck and slipped into the first patch of shadow she found. It was under a swivel gun.

'Oi, new rat,' said the three-legged stranger. 'Phew, you move fast!'

He stood in the light, quite fearless.

'Leave me be,' said Rip. She had trouble catching her breath. Her sides heaved. Where was she? How could she get back to her sisters? She crouched, ready for battle.

'We don't want to fight,' said the second rat, the one with a blotch over one side of his face.

Rip looked at him with wide eyes.

'Are you sure?'

'Yes.'

'*Kree*?' said Rip.

'Eh?' said the first rat.

'That might be her name,' said the second rat. 'Is it your name?'

'No. I'm called Rip,' she said. Her ears went down and she relaxed. 'Don't you know what *kree* means?'

'No. I am Peg and this is Patch,' said the three-legged rat.

'*Kree* means peace,' said Rip. 'It means a few more things, too.'

'Like what?' said Patch.

'Did your mum rat not teach you these things?'

'We don't have a mum rat,' said Peg.

Rip looked at him, perplexed.

'Is it a kind of pi-rat?' said Patch.

'I don't know what that is,' said Rip.

'We are pi-rats,' said Peg, proudly. 'We are free! We roam the seas. We take what we want. We do as we please.'

It all made sense to Rip now. No one had taught her new friends how to behave. They were fearless because they'd never learned to be afraid.

'That sounds good,' said Rip, 'but I must get back to my sis Lu and sis Preen. They are my best friends.'

'Like me and Patch,' said Peg.

'But they are over there,' said Rip. 'The sea is in the way.'

'What can you do?' said Patch.

Rip settled onto her stomach.

'I don't know,' she said. Her whiskers drooped.

Rip had never been without her sisters. One or the other had been close to her since they were tiny. She missed them, badly.

'Don't be sad,' said Peg. 'Join us. Drink, eat, sleep and have fun.'

Part of Rip thought that was a very bad idea. She was a serious, steady rat. Then again, she was tired of being sensible all the time.

'Fine,' she said. 'Show me how.'

'Great!' said Patch.

The brothers were as good as their word. They showed Rip the whole of the barque. It didn't take long as the ship was smaller than the *Hydromyst*. It was also much narrower as it was built for speed rather than cargo.

The biggest difference between the two ships was that this one had a gun deck. At first, Rip stayed away as there were Big pirates all over it, moving cannons around, lifting iron and picking up barrels of gunpowder. They did this last thing very, very carefully.

The pirates had rigged up a winch on the *Hydromyst* and were lifting some of the heavy weapons over from the barque. Eventually, all the heaving, clanking and cursing stopped and Patch led Rip in to look.

The three rats climbed all over the pyramids made of cannon balls. One rolled out of place, narrowly missing Peg's front paw.

'Oops,' he said, with a jaunty flick of his ears. 'Not this time.'

The merriness of the two brothers, who played hide and seek and touch-my-tail, began to make Rip feel a bit better. She watched them pounce and bounce about.

'Come and play!' said Peg.

'I'm not good at play time,' said Rip. 'I like to stay still.'

'Oh come on,' said Patch. 'Chase me!'

He ran up the rounded spine of a cannon and paused at the top to make a rude noise.

Rip sprinted after him.

'Whee!' He jumped off and skittered away.

Rip reached the muzzle of the cannon. Instead of jumping, she clambered into the tube. The metal walls were slightly warm from the sun. She snuffled her way down to the bottom, turned awkwardly and climbed back out. Her fur acted like a duster. She emerged covered in soot and oil.

'Swiff!' she sneezed.

Peg laughed. 'You are a mess.' It was his turn to run away. After teasing Rip for a while, the brothers decided it was time for dinner.

'This way,' said Peg. He showed her to a cabin. It had a rich, soft rug on the floor and it smelled of lily perfume. There was a vanity table with a mirror and a wardrobe stocked with mothballs.

'Here,' said Patch. He swaggered over to a plate in the corner. It held a meal of boiled potatoes and chicken. The rats devoured it then drank from a bowl of water.

Round-tummied, Rip felt sleepy. She went to digest beneath the bunk bed.

Blanche walked into the cabin, her heels clicking against the planks. The lady pirate sighed and sat down at the dressing table. She used a damp cloth to take off her makeup, removed her wig and shook her hair free. It hung down her back in a long tangle. She stood to change her clothing.

Rip stayed hidden but Peg and Patch ran around in the pile of cloth.

'Hello, boys,' said the Big. 'Oh, it's wonderful to get that dress off.'

Rip flattened herself. Peg and Patch obviously though they were safe because they tumbled over Blanche's feet. She spoke to them.

'Have you had your dinner? Good lads.'

She shrugged them gently off her feet and put on a loose blouse and breeches. Patch swarmed up her leg, up her shirt and tugged on her collar.

'And a good day to you, too!' said Blanche. She offered a flat palm to the rat, who stepped onto it. She put him on her shoulder, where other pirates might let a parrot perch.

Rip watched nervously. There was a knock at the door. 'Yes?'

'There's someone from our new ship here to see you,' said the pirate outside.

'Come in,' said Blanche.

Rip stepped back, retreating further into the shadows. She liked having something solid over her head.

But the Big who came through the door was familiar. It was Runa. Rip's nose quivered. The girl smelled of fear but there was a current of determination running like cool water through warm.

'*Bonjour, madam Fleur*,' said Runa, and Blanche nodded.

'Good day,' she replied, also in French. 'What brings you over to the *Liberté*?'

'I want to be a pirate,' said Runa. 'I saw Abel. He's the same age as me. If he can do it so can I. I'm a girl, but so are you.'

'Abel is part of our crew because he has nowhere else to go, my pretty. Is it the same for you?'

'No,' said Runa. 'I was on my way home when you captured my ship. I won't see my father for months.

That's why I need to talk to you. I want to be a pirate but only for a short time, please.'

Blanche was amused.

'Is your father rich, little girl?'

Actually, Runa's father was very well off but Runa had the good sense to say 'no.'

'Then you are no use to us as a ransom,' said Blanche. 'And yet, I wonder if you truly know what you are asking. Do you understand what pirates are?'

'You are bloodthirsty killers,' said Runa, enthusiastically. 'You are the scourge of the sea. You take what you want and answer to no man.'

Blanche threw her head back and laughed.

Runa became thoughtful.

'I don't want to kill anyone,' she said. 'Not if you let me be a short-term pirate. Though I would like to learn how to use a sword and how to swash and buckle.'

Blanche patted Runa's shoulder.

'Girl, I will tell you what we truly are. We are hunted. We are hated. We are feared. If ever we were caught by the navy of any country they would hang us at once. How old are you?'

'I am eleven, almost twelve.'

'That's an awful lot of life to lose out on if something goes wrong.'

'But you won't get caught, though,' said Runa. 'And if you do, I will pretend I was your prisoner.'

Blanche laughed again.

'There may be a bit of buccaneer in you after all,' she said, reaching up to tickle Patch.

'I like your rat,' said Runa. 'That's how I knew you weren't one of the really bad pirates.'

'Oh? You aren't scared?'

'No,' said Runa. 'I have my own ratty.'

'These boys are special to me,' said Blanche, scratching Patch between the ears. 'When I came to this ship they were the only two left. They were tiny. I fed them by hand. They are misunderstood.'

'I agree,' said Runa, eagerly. 'Will they be safe without me?'

'My beloved Rouge is a Benin warrior-woman. She taught me everything I know about sailing and I taught her everything I know about navigation. She is a good captain. Your rat friends will be fine.'

'Phew,' said Runa.

'Very well. You are a hostage here, but you can have the run of the ship and you will be part of my crew except in name. That way if we are captured then you will not be hanged as a pirate. But you must not get in the way of the senior pirates and you must follow any orders. Follow Abel and he will show you your duties.'

'Aye-aye,' said Runa.

'Dismissed.'

Runa went to the door and paused. She turned back. Rip poked her nose out from under the bed.

'Captain Blanche,' the girl said. 'You won't hurt the old Captain and the Bosun, will you? They were good to me.'

Blanche's face went grim. Runa fled.

# Chapter 4: How to be a Pirat

That night, the pirates had a party. One had an accordion, another a violin and a third beat out a rhythm on a drum. They toasted the beginning of their pirate fleet. They renamed the *Hydromyst*. From now on it would be called the *Black Caesar*. Both ships floated side-by-side – close enough for Rip to smell her friends, but much too far for her to leap across.

It was a merry evening. The men danced, looping their arms to turn and leap about while Rouge and Blanche danced together. Runa joined in but Abel sat alone at the edge of the lamplight. When the stars came out, he disappeared.

Rip also stayed away. Patch and Peg danced on their back legs for scraps but she didn't like the crowded deck.

She found a ratline and clambered up the rigging. Rip rose past the fighting top and the sails until she came to the high lookout basket at the top of the mast.

Abel was already up there, sitting quietly on his knees, looking out over the sea. The water behind the barque shone a magical blue-green as the hull tickled a bloom of algae so it glowed. Starlight glimmered on the edges of the waves.

The young Big was so still and silent Rip knew he hadn't seen her.

She didn't disturb him. She just sat on the edge of the basket, equally as quiet and thoughtful.

After a while, Abel started singing. It was very different from the shanties Rip heard from below. This was a song of sorrow and the boy kept his voice low and gentle. It was not a bad sound. For some reason, it made Rip think of her home nest, which lay on the other side of the ocean.

When the song ended, Abel sighed and turned around to climb down.

He saw Rip.

Rip froze.

The Big froze too.

They stayed, still and staring at each other, for a long time. Then Rip sneezed. She flung her legs out and went: '*Swiff! Swiff!*'

Abel scrambled back so fast he almost fell out of the basket. He put his legs over the side and dropped out of view.

Rip sat quivering from nose to tail. The Big had been *terrified* of her.

This was very strange. He was easily a hundred times bigger than Rip.

All wild rats learn to be wary of humans, though some were like Lu, who was a mixture of brave and daft, or Peg and Patch who didn't know better. Rip was used to the idea Bigs hated rats, but she'd never seen a human run from a rat before.

Rip felt strong and scary all of a sudden.

The party calmed down. One by one the pirates and their new crew members went below-decks. The musicians packed up.

Rip climbed down to the weather deck. Peg and Patch, unlike the pirates, were still wide-awake and bright-eyed.

'Hey rat boys,' said Rip. She had an idea.

'Hi Rip.'

'Who is the Skip of this ship?' said Rip.

'What is a Skip?' said Peg.

'The rat in charge, the one who says what to do and when it should be done.'

Peg looked at Patch uncertainly.

'Our Big?' he said.

Rip hissed quietly.

'What do Bigs know about rat life? You don't even know *kree*.'

'Teach us,' said Patch.

So Rip told them:

*You must know the rules of kree*
*If you want to live with me.*
*You should sniff-sniff to say hi,*
*Bear no grudges if you fight*
*Always look out for your friends*
*Keep your word, as is right.*
*Now you know the rules of kree*
*So we can live well, you and me.*

'You have been on your own too long,' said Rip. 'You need to learn how to be a wild rat.'

'Fine,' said Peg. 'Let's make it fair. If you teach us what you know, we will show you how to be a pi-rat.'

'Done,' said Rip. 'Now, for the first thing, where do pi-rats nap?'

'We'll show you,' said Patch.

The boys led her to the corner of the cabin where someone had nailed pieces of cloth to the walls to make little hammocks. Peg climbed in first by standing on Patch's shoulders. Rip jumped in and wobbled as the hammock swayed.

'This is the best thing I have seen in my whole life,' she declared as she curled up cosy. 'I love it.'

Over the next few days, Rip showed the boys all the skills a wild rat needs. She showed them how to steal, sneak, climb up high and swim in a bucket full of water. They became so skilled they could pinch a biscuit from under the nose of a ruthless pirate. The only thing she didn't do was show them how to fight.

They still went back to their bowl of food because no self-respecting rat would turn their nose up at an easy meal. They got a lot of exercise thieving and trespassing.

It still felt strange to have the whole ship to themselves. Rip sometimes caught old scent trails left by the rats that had once been there. They were very faint.

By the end of this, Rip felt like a big sister once more. It didn't make up for missing Lu and Preen, but she felt a little better.

In return, Peg and Patch showed Rip the life of a pi-rat. They rampaged around the *Liberté*, climbing and wrestling. They took Rip to every nook and cranny of the barque and showed her all the best places to gnaw and nibble. They shared all the games they knew, like race-to-the-scuppers, play dead and sniff-chase. Rip, who used to think games were a waste of time, found herself getting quite good at them.

Sometimes Rip saw Runa working alongside Abel, scrubbing the deck or splicing ropes. The girl smelled hearty and fit. She chatted happily to Abel and didn't seem to mind the boy never replied.

Rip did not go near them. She stayed hidden when the pirates gathered on deck to listen to their captain. The woman in white stood on the top deck, her hair blowing in the wind.

'Friends,' she called. 'We have a choice. We can stay around the Indies or we can sail south to safety.'

'Times have changed,' said one pirate. 'There are fewer sea rovers and more naval ships in these waters.'

'But the hunting is better in these parts,' said another.

In the end, they cast a vote and decided to stay for one more raid before turning to the open sea.

'To freedom!' said Captain Blanche.

'To freedom!' roared her crew.

They sailed on, the *Liberté* stalking the sea lanes for victims, the *Hydromyst* ploughing on behind her, slow but steady. It only had four cannons and Captain Rouge had no intention of taking her into battle.

Then someone spotted a ship on the horizon and everything changed.

# Chapter 5: Hunting

'Ready the crew,' Captain Blanche said to her first mate.

'Aye Captain.'

The sails dropped and canvas bulged and snapped as it filled with wind. The pirates turned the wheel and carved out a new path with the rudder.

Rip, Peg and Patch, lying in their hammocks, lifted their heads. They sensed the ship change direction and pick up speed.

'Get off me,' said Peg, who was using his brother as a duvet. 'There will be a Big fight. Let's go and watch.'

The rats tumbled out of their beds. Rip scampered along with the brothers.

The pirates were scrambling into position.

This time, the distressed damsel trick would not work. The other ship was sailing away from them and showed no signs of wanting to get close. The *Liberté's* only option was a swift attack.

The crew of the other ship spotted the pirates coming. Rip could hear the faint cries of officers giving orders.

'It's a race,' said Peg.

The *Liberté* skimmed the waves. The wind was on their side. Captain Blanche set a course to meet the other ship at an angle.

The fleeing captain realised this. Rip and the two boys squinted to see but the other vessel was too far away.

It was thrilling for Rip to take part in a hunt. She could hear, smell and feel the excitement.

'Go fast, go fast!' chittered Peg.

'Catch them, catch them!' said Patch. He ground his teeth with impatience.

The prey moved off course. The enemy ship angled itself and trimmed its sails to take advantage of the same wind that pushed the *Liberté* along. Now they were closer, it was clear this was a massive, full-rigged ship with four masts. Now it ran directly ahead of them. The *Liberté* was lighter and smaller so it needed less wind, but this new ship had a huge spread of canvas. Perhaps it could outrun them.

Rip put her paws against the wood and stretched up to look out. The ship was a growing blur to her. They were catching up.

'She has no cannon, Cap'n,' said the pirate first mate.

'We'll show them ours then,' said Captain Blanche. 'Go broadside.'

The *Liberté* was right on the heels of the other ship. This close, the pirates were taking the wind out of its sails. The *Liberté* swung round and Rip heard the crack-slam of the gun ports as they were flung open.

Captain Blanche hailed the other skipper in French.

'Ahoy!' she shouted. 'Will you let us board or shall we cripple you first?'

The new ship, which was called the *Amitié*, was within range.

'Go and drink bilge-water, pirate scum!' shouted their captain.

'I think that meant no,' said the first mate.

'In that case, fire,' said Captain Blanche, very calmly.

'Fire!' shouted the first mate.

'Fire!' shouted the second mate down on the gun deck.

Half-a-dozen flames touched a half-a-dozen fuses. Five muzzles flashed as five iron balls flew through the air.

'Bum,' said one pirate. 'Sorry, one moment...'

By then, the first thunderblast had died away. Two of the cannonballs splashed into the sea but three struck home. They slammed into the side of the *Amitié*. One smashed into the rigging, snapping spars and ropes.

Rip thought the whole world had exploded. Her brain felt as though it had been squashed flat by the noise. Her nose burned with sharp-smelling smoke.

'Do you surrender?' said Captain Blanche.

'No! May your scurvy bones end up as fish-food, unnatural female!'

'Are you sure?'

'I will see you hang, Haitian demon-woman!'

'Very well,' said Captain Blanche. 'Reload and prepare to...'

Just then the last cannon went off. The ball sailed through the air, crashed through the deck and buried itself in the bowels of the *Amitié*. The hole it left stopped less than a metre from the captain's feet. The breeze from its passing ruffled his wig.

'Oops,' said a voice from the gun deck.

'We surrender,' said the other captain, very quickly.

'Grappling hooks,' said Blanche. Her first mate nodded. Suddenly, the deck swarmed with pirates.

Rip watched them throw ropes with hooks on the end across the gap between the ships. Some of them caught on the railings and the pirates started to haul the lines.

'Heave,' shouted Captain Blanche.

'Ho,' shouted her men.

'Meep,' said Rip as the ship shuddered. It swung closer to the captured vessel.

'Come on, Rip,' said Patch. 'Now we board the ship!'

The gap closed. The *Amitié* was taller than the *Liberté*, so it was a risky business for the pirates to climb aboard. For the rats, though, it was a easy. No one noticed Patch, Peg and Rip fling themselves onto the strange deck.

The pirates tied up the merchant crew. Blanche had no intention of taking the ship, which was far too large to crew. Instead, she raided it.

Peg tripped over to a hatch and slithered through the grating.

The pirates were looking for gold, velvets and other treasures but the rats were after a different kind of booty.

'I smell something sweet,' said Rip. 'It's fruit.'

She followed her nose to the captain's cabin. She jumped onto the desk, kicked over a crystal ink pot and sent a silver letter-opener spinning. She left footprints all over the expensive carpet and stopped for a wee on one of the captain's posh, pink-powdered wigs.

Finally, she found what she was looking for: a box of cake. She sniffed carefully and then dived in. Patch joined in.

Soon the rats had eaten so much that Rip felt as though there was a cannonball in her belly. They staggered off to find Peg.

He was in the hold and he had an audience.

Strange rats milled around, scattering when a pirate stamped his way to the cargo.

'We are on a raid,' said Peg. 'Give us all your stuff!'

He was bouncing on his three legs, his eyes flashing.

Rip was not so happy. She sniffed. There was a smell in the hold. It filled her nostrils, rank, thick and nasty. It scared her but she also wanted to find out what it was.

'Get off our ship,' said a tan-furred buck rat. 'My stuff is my stuff. Go and get your own.'

'*You* go and get stuff for me!' said Peg, stubbornly.

Rip took the opportunity to sneak off. She tiptoed past crates and stacks of goods. The smell grew stronger. It was made up of bitter sweat and bad feelings. It came from a group of Bigs in a caged-off section of the hold. A single lantern cast shadows that spread and shrank as it swung overhead.

There was a mixture of women, men and children. They weren't wearing very much. This did not strike Rip as odd as she thought the Big habit of dressing in cloth was strange. They did, though, all have metal things around their necks. Rip's nose twitched. She thought they smelled wrong, not ill, nor drunk like a sailor... this was something worse. They had not been allowed to eat, clean themselves, breathe good air or see sunlight for far too long. It reminded her of the strange, hulking ship she had sniffed several nights ago.

Suddenly, a Big swept over Rip, her skirts swaying, her legs stretching up like vast columns. It was Captain Blanche.

'More tobacco,' she boomed, annoyed. 'And cotton. We can't sell it to the English mills. Nor will there be much point in trading it back to the United States. It would be like selling cider to an apple-grower. What's through here?'

The rat crouched beside the pirate, whisking her whiskers.

Captain Blanche suddenly went very quiet and still.

'Fetch the captain,' she said.

# Chapter 6: Horror in the Hold

The skipper of the *Amitié* was dragged down to the hold. His wig was askew and his face was a mess of white powder. He stood, trembling, before Captain Blanche.

'Open the door,' she said.

'Madam, he said. 'I have a contract to keep.'

Captain Blanche said something very rude about his contract and where he could shove it.

'Open the door,' she said, again. This time she lifted her cutlass and pointed it at the cage.

The other captain fumbled with a set of keys. He turned one in the lock.

'Strike the irons from them,' said Blanche with icy calm.

'I can't let you do that,' the captain waffled. 'They aren't my property.'

'They aren't anyone's *property*!'

Rip knew something bad was likely to happen to the ship. She felt like a great storm was coming.

Someone came running with a hammer and chisel and started to free the chained Bigs.

Rip didn't watch. What Bigs did was none of her concern. But Peg and Patch were still aboard and so was she.

Rip ran, her head and tail held low. She went at speed through the hold to the hatch. On the way she passed Patch and Peg who were still trying to bully the new rats. It wasn't working.

'Why should we give you our food?' one of the bemused rats was saying.

'You have to! We are pi-rats,' squeaked Peg. 'It's just how it works.'

'Yeah,' said Patch.

'But *why*?'

'Hey,' said Rip, but they ignored her. She felt prickly all over. The bad feeling grew and became a terrible feeling. Her skin twitched and her ears and eyes stretched with anxiety.

'Do it,' urged Peg.

'Make me,' said the new rat.

The argument went on and Rip decided she couldn't wait for it to end. She nipped Patch on the rump.

'Ow,' he said. 'Why did you bite me?'

'Stop all this right now,' said Rip. 'We must leave.'

She saw dozens of blinking eyes and puzzled faces. No one moved.

'This ship could sink,' she said. 'We must go now.'

'Where?' said a fat-bellied rat. She looked like she was ready to have a litter of babies.

'To our ship,' said Rip. 'It is safe. We can't stay here.'

The new rats were scared by the thudding of boxes and boots. There was too much shouting and too many strange things happening. Rip could tell they were close to panic.

'Come with me,' she said. 'I'll show you the way. Patch and Peg, you go last. They can't lag. Make sure not one rat is left here. Now move!'

Rip ran.

The rats followed. They travelled in a wedge-shape with Rip racing at the front. More rats joined them.

The furry little herd scrambled up to the weather deck. Rip sprinted for the side of the ship. She propelled herself up and perched on the balustrade to lean over. Like all rats, her eyesight was not good and she wasn't sure if the *Liberté* was waiting below.

The other rats piled behind her.

'Where now?' said one buck.

'Jump down to the small ship,' said Rip. 'It's close but I'm not sure where. We have to leap.'

She bunched up to spring. All around them, pirates were throwing the last few valuables aboard. One rolled a barrel of salt pork across the deck. He lifted it over the side. Hands reached up to catch it.

'Stop!' a rat squeaked. 'Don't move.'

Rip quivered, her muscles ready to launch.

The speaker was a pale rat. He emerged from the pack. He was long, thin and seemed to be in charge.

'Why have you made us stop?' said Rip.

'This is our home,' he said. Carefully, he put himself between Rip and the drop down to the other ship.

'Your home will sink!' said Rip. 'Move!'

'Tell her we won't go,' said another rat, a quite ordinary-looking female with a shrill voice.

The Bigs were removing the grappling hooks. They pushed at the hull of the other ship, some with poles, others with their bare hands.

'There is no time!' said Rip.

She barrelled toward the strange buck rat. Her shoulder collided with his side and they both fell. For a long moment, she tumbled through the air, her tail whirling like a propeller as she tried to keep upright. She hit the deck and the impact drove the wind from her lungs. She was back on the *Liberté*.

The blond rat was next to her. He was winded too. Other rats dropped like ripe apples.

They encircled Rip and milled around. The blond rat stood up and shook his head, dazed.

Peg and Patch pushed through the crowd.

'Hi Rip,' said Peg. 'We got all the rats here.'

Rip squatted wild-eyed on the deck.

'We made it,' she said.

Over their heads, the sails dropped and the *Liberté* started to pull away from the *Amitié*.

The rats were whispering. They passed a message on with tiny movements of their ears and whiskers.

'She beat Gold,' they said. 'She beat him!'

One by one, they ventured forward to sniff-sniff Rip respectfully – all but a handful who stayed back.

'I think you are the boss rat now,' chirped Patch.

'I can't be,' said Rip. 'I am a doe.'

'Why would that stop you?' said Peg.

The Bigs were shouting again. Rip crouched down just as the cannons fired. The whole vessel juddered. The other ship fared worse. The cannonballs couldn't miss at this range. They smashed into the hull. They crashed into the masts. They splintered wood and buckled the deck. The *Amitié* started to sink.

The rats scattered so they didn't see how quickly it happened. One minute there was a ship, battered but seaworthy, sitting on the surface of the ocean. The next moment it wallowed, its prow dipping beneath the waves. Then, inch by inch, it slid under the water. The stern was the last part to slip out of sight. Bubbles, scraps of wood and flotsam floated to the top.

A small boat also bobbed around in the swirl of jetsam. The crew of the *Amitié* had seized just enough time to launch their lifeboat from the far side of the sinking ship and row away.

Captain Blanche stood on the deck. Her sharp eyes caught the fleeing boat.

'They are still in range, ma'am,' said her first mate. 'Shall we fire another volley?'

Captain Blanche stared at the little boat with its pale, worried crew and its sculling oars. It was overloaded and vulnerable, though not far from the coast.

'Ma'am?'

Captain Blanche said nothing.

'Ma'am, they're escaping.'

'Hold fire,' the captain said, quietly but firmly.

# Chapter 7: Rip the Skip

The two ships anchored up, leaving a wide gap between them because of the choppy water. The *Liberté* and the *Black Caesar* had found each other near the coast of Brazil. The huge country was under the control of the Portuguese Empire.

'I will not land here,' said Captain Blanche when she met Rouge in her cabin. Rip, who had her head in Patch and Peg's food bowl, listened to the human voices boom above her. She was more interested in the scraps of hard bread than the Bigs, even though the two women were deciding her fate.

'Aye,' said Rouge. 'It's too risky. They buy and sell folk here, too.'

'Spanish ships patrol to the North. There are English and Portuguese fleets here too,' said Captain Blanche. The two women pored over a chart of the shipping routes and settlements. Rip finished eating and went to lie in her hammock for a snooze.

'Where can we sell the loot, then?' said Rouge. 'Coffee growers don't need coffee. Tobacco farmers don't want for tobacco.'

'There is one place we might make a good profit,' said Captain Blanche. 'And we can make the Dutch flag and sailors work for us.'

'Where?'

'The Silver Empire,' said Captain Blanche. 'Japan. They smoke and they might want coffee. I'm sure we have someone here who can forge the papers.'

'Great idea,' said Captain Rouge, with clear admiration. 'They must regret the day you escaped your shackles and joined the rebellion.'

'They did,' said Captain Blanche. She pointed at the map. 'Whatever happens, we meet up here on the isle of Tokudaia.'

'Agreed.'

'I will miss you.'

'And I you.'

\*\*\*\*\*

Rip woke to find she had a crew of her own to deal with.

The first clue was rustling sounds and a chorus of cheeping. She popped her head over the side of the hammock and sniff-sniffed. Then she opened her eyes.

Half a dozen of the new rats squatted on the floor.

'Skip, where should we hide?' said one rat.

'Boss rat, what can we eat?' said another.

'Rip, tell us where it is safe to go.'

'Where do we find things to make our nests?'

'Are the Bigs bad here?'

'Can I stash this?'

'Who gets the best place to sleep?'

'What will you do if one of us rats does the wrong thing?'

Rip blinked and yawned. Clearly being Skip was not as simple as just giving out orders.

'Stay down low,' she said. 'The Bigs here do not use traps yet but they might some day. Eat from the things the Bigs throw out. Er…'

The questions kept coming. Rip was used to being in charge of her sisters so she tried to answer every one. Soon she was hungry and still the questions came.

Eventually, the rats went away, all except the big blond rat she had bashed into the day before.

'I'm Gold,' he said.

'What do you want?' she said.

'I want you!' said Gold. 'I like you.'

'Oh, get lost,' said Rip.

'Please?'

'No.'

Rip jumped out of her hammock and went to the bowl to check for food. Someone else had eaten it all. She ground her teeth, annoyed. She ignored Gold who tried to sniff-sniff with her.

'Ugh,' said Rip. The day had not started well.

It did not improve.

Everywhere she went, rats popped up to sniff-sniff with her. It took ages to get anywhere. A clutch of little rittens who hadn't yet learned *kree* or rat politeness followed her around tugging at her tail and clutching at her fur.

'Leave me be!' squeaked Rip.

Being the boss of two sisters was a pain. Being the boss of dozens of rats was far worse. She tried to hide but the rats followed her scent and found her wherever she went. It was impossible to sleep.

By dusk, Rip was fed up. She just wanted to be alone. But Patch and Peg appeared.

'Hi Rip,' said Peg. 'How is it, being Skip?'

'Bad,' said Rip. 'Why can't I have some peace from them?'

'You saved them,' said Patch. 'They think they need you.'

The only good thing about being Skip, as far as Rip could see, was that she could eat from all the food stashes. She wondered how Old Pew, the skip on the ship once known as the *Hydromyst*, got the rats to leave him alone. Perhaps she would have to be scary like Black Spot, the Skip rat who had ruled before Pew.

Night-time was as busy as the day.

'This rat bit me,' one rat complained.

'My food stash has gone,' said another.

'A Big saw me and got cross!' said a third.

Rip tried to give the best advice. It was hard because the new rats were used to having more space on a bigger ship. They squabbled and fought.

Rip worried the Bigs would realise they were suddenly sharing their space with loads of rats. Her Mum Rat warned her Bigs were not good at sharing.

The next day, Rip was tired and unhappy.

Gold found her sulking in a corner.

'Hi Rip,' he said. 'Be my wife.'

'No,' said Rip.

'Why not?'

'I just don't want to.'

'What do you want?'

'To be left in peace. Gold, I want you to be boss rat, not me.'

'No thanks,' said Gold. 'Life is more fun when you don't have to be in charge.'

'I'll fight you and make you say you will be the boss,' Rip warned, puffing up.

'You are so smart and strong,' said Gold, who clearly wasn't interested in fighting. 'You would be a great wife.'

Rip grew angry. She didn't enjoy politics, but raging at Gold would do no good. She couldn't make another rat the leader by beating them up or by begging.

Gold tried to comb her fur with his teeth to show his friendly feelings but she shrugged him off.

'I don't want to be your wife,' she said. 'I have to go now.'

She climbed to the only place she could think might be private; up to the basket on the middle mast.

Abel was already there and so was Runa.

'Ugh,' said Rip. '*Bigs*. At least you won't ask me things all the time or try to lick me.' She decided to stay, but then Abel saw her.

He started shaking. Runa put her arms around his shoulders. His face shone with wetness and he sobbed. Runa took a hanky from her pocket and offered it to him.

'What's wrong?' she said, in French. 'Are you ill?'

Abel shook his head.

'What then?'

The boy stretched out his hand and pointed. Rip looked up at the tip of a finger.

'Oh, it's all the rats,' said Runa. 'Yes, there are rather a lot now, but they won't hurt you. You are about a hundred times as big as that ratty. I think she's as scared of you as you are of her.'

Abel opened his mouth. He closed it again. A small noise came out. Rip and Runa were both as still as statues.

'We were in chains,' said the boy. His voice sounded creaky like a door hinge that hadn't been used.

'Yes?' said Runa, very gently.

'The rats came. We couldn't get away. It was dark. I could feel them on me.'

Runa put her hand on Abel's. His rested on the rim of the basket.

'That won't happen again, not if I can help it,' she said.

'What can you do?'

'You can come home with me. I'll tell Pappa how you protected me from the pirates, how you were my best friend apart from white ratty. He'll have to let you stay with us, but only if you want to.'

'You were friends with a rat?' said Abel.

'Oh yes.'

'Are we friends?'

'I'd like to think so,' said Runa. 'You helped me learn how to splice ropes and swab the decks. I don't mind if you don't speak so much. I speak more than I should. Pappa says it would be a boring world if we were all the same.'

Abel smiled. This was a rare thing. His face shone.

Rip took advantage of how the Bigs kept the other rats away. She washed herself, enjoying her own company. It was good to escape being pestered. She groomed her face, arms, flank and bottom. The boy Big was okay, she decided. He wasn't trying to poke or prod her.

Abel's smile faded. He shaded his eyes with a flat hand.

'What is it?' said Runa.

Abel seemed to have lost his voice again. He pointed at a dot on the horizon.

'A ship,' said Runa. 'I'll tell Captain Blanche.'

'Quick,' said Abel.

# Chapter 8: Race for Freedom

Runa shinned down the mast. She was a quick climber now.

When she alerted the first mate, he whipped out a telescope. His face turned pale.

'It's a Portuguese ship,' he said. 'From the colours they are flying, I'd guess it's a pirate-hunter.'

Word got around fast. Captain Blanche strode up to the weather deck.

'The crew we fired on got to shore and raised the alarm, then,' she said.

'What about the *Hydromyst*? She's slower than us,' said Runa.

'The *Black Caesar*, don't you mean? Fly our pirate flag,' said the captain. 'Let's give them a chase. They might ignore her and come after us. We look like buccaneers but they look like a merchant ship.'

'Aye Ma'am.'

The black and white flag unfurled. They kept the sails cinched in tight and waited. As the pursuers got closer, it became clear they were sailing a 62-gunner. It was far more powerful than the *Liberté*.

'These seas will be crawling with enemies soon,' said Captain Blanche. 'Let's give them a good run.'

She ordered the pirates to reduce the sails as though they had been damaged. The pirates, careful not to sail at full speed, set a zig-zagging course that kept the *Liberté* dancing ahead of the relentless Portuguese ship.

For the next day and night, the pirates played a dangerous game, sailing back and forth across the deep blue waters, showing themselves to every crew they came near. Soon they were being trailed by a flotilla of enemy ships. Captain Blanche was luring them away from the *Black Caesar*.

It was a tricky and risky tactic. If the *Liberté* got trapped between two ships, then they would be captured.

The Portuguese fleet tried to trap the pirates the way wolves hunt deer. They tried to sail up in a pincer movement and pushed the *Liberté* this way and that. They attempted to steal the wind from their sails and they sent out the smallest and fastest ships to catch her. When dusk fell, they doused their lights and tried to sneak up on the pirates. But Captain Blanche was wily and determined. She slipped out of the ambushes and outpaced the enemy.

None of the pirates slept more than an hour at a time. Runa and Abel were kept busy as lookouts, peering with tired eyes to spot any danger.

Meanwhile, Rip had her own problems. She didn't know the ship was under threat from a navy but she sensed the tension in the crew and it scared her. Her biggest trouble, though, was the other rats.

They would not stop squabbling. They stole, they nagged her and they left droppings everywhere. Once, she woke up in her hammock to find three rats nibbling her fur. She made an annoyed sound.

'We are here to clean you,' said one.

'I can clean my own fur,' said Rip.

'But it's a sign you are in charge,' said another. 'We want to help our boss rat.'

Rip struggled free. She knew if she let them wash her as a sign of respect then very soon she would have bald patches.

Gold found her sitting in a grumpy little huddle at the prow of the ship. Peg and Patch were with her. They couldn't stop giggling when Rip told them what happened.

'I'll chase you off,' Rip warned them all, but they were interrupted when a trio of rats rolled across the deck in an angry, struggling ball.

'I hate you!'

'Give it to me!'

'No, it's mine!' they squeaked.

Rip waded in to break up the fight. She bit one, cuffed another and sat down on the third.

'Be quiet,' she said. 'Get out of sight, now.'

The three young rats scurried off.

'What is wrong with them?' she said to the others. Peg and Patch shrugged.

'There are lots of us,' said Gold. 'That's what's wrong. There are loads of rats and not much space.'

'This is not good,' sniffed Rip.

She decided to check through the ship to see what else was happening. There was plenty of trouble belowdecks. The rats were running rampant. They pushed each other out of hiding-places, tussled and argued in loud shrieks. One of the does made a nest and now six little baby rittens lay snuggled up to her. She looked at Rip with big, anxious eyes.

'Rip, help us. It's all too much,' said the new mum. 'I'm scared in case a fight breaks out here and we get hurt.'

'I will tell them to stop,' said Rip. 'Just take care and be well, you and your young ones.'

The mother smiled, relaxing her ears.

As they moved on, Gold said: 'We would have good, strong young if you were my wife.'

'Now is not a good time!' Rip snapped. 'The ship is too full. We don't need more rats.'

Gold wilted.

'You are right,' he said, crestfallen. 'I am wrong.'

Rip looked at him. He wasn't a bad rat; she just wasn't interested in him.

'Don't ask me again, please,' she said.

'No, Rip. I won't.'

'What can we do about this?' Rip sighed, looking at the chaos. Bad things happened when there were too many rats. The food would run out. Even worse, if the Bigs noticed there were too many rats then they would be in real trouble. When Bigs declared war on rats, lives would be lost.

Rip went right into the middle of the hold, climbed up a wooden crate and stood on top, balancing on her back legs. Then she made the loudest squeak she could.

'Shut up, you lot!'

The squabbling rats turned to her. She felt nervous looking down at hundreds of faces.

'Can all of you hear me? Good,' she said. 'We need to stop this now. If you keep on this way, then the Bigs will get sick of us and that would be bad news. We need some new rules to help us stay safe.'

'We don't need more rules,' said one rat. It was a female and she clicked her teeth together disrespectfully. 'We have *kree*.'

'*Kree* will not do the job,' said Rip. 'Not now with things the way they are. This ship is too small for us. We must take care. We need to stash food and eat a bit less so we don't starve. We have to keep out of sight and make less noise. We can't fight all the time.'

'Why not?' said the rat.

'If the Bigs think our group is too large then they will kill us,' said Rip. 'Why do you think there were just two rats on the ship when you got here? They have done it once, they can do it again.'

Some of the rats seemed to agree, but Rip heard a few chitters and grumbles. The rat who had spoken earlier did not look impressed.

'This is for our own good,' said Rip. 'From now on, if you want to fight, come to me first. I will sort it out.'

'You just want to boss us round,' said another rat.

'No, I don't,' said Rip. She was not sure they believed her.

'When will these new rules stop?' said a third rat.

Rip said, 'When we are safe.'

There was more ratty grumbling.

Rip climbed down from the box and re-joined her friends. The other rats scattered. They went quietly, which was a relief.

'Not all of them like what you said,' said Peg.

Gold said, 'Some of them know what you said was smart. It's good you care. Some Skips don't care. They just do what they want. But the best boss rats are the ones who do what they *have* to do to help.'

'Do you think I did the right thing?' said Rip.

'We will have to find out,' said Patch.

'This is hard work,' said Rip. 'I don't want to be Skip.'

'Nor did I,' said Gold. 'I'd watch out if I were you. Don't trust the rats not on your side.'

'What are their names?' said Rip.

'The doe who spoke first is called Spite. She has lots of friends, like Sneak, Sharp, Swipe, Slink, Stink, Snap and Twitch, who is small. Take care with them, Rip.'

'I will.'

That night, the pirates had a narrow escape. The wind dropped, which made all the ships slow down. When the night was at its deepest and darkest, the pursuers launched a little fleet of boats. They covered their lanterns and rowed by starlight, hoping to board the *Liberté* and take the pirates by surprise.

They tried to be quiet but Abel heard the sound of oars in the water and rang a bell to warn the crew. Instantly, the pirates drew their swords and loaded their muskets.

'Retreat, retreat!' called the Portuguese captain as the guns cracked and shots whizzed over their heads.

Captain Blanche, who had been sleeping, strode onto the deck as fresh and determined as always.

'The wind has risen. Sail full and by with all speed.'

'Aye cap'n.'

The *Liberté* took the wind and shot forward as if unleashed. She pulled away from the bigger ships and left the small boats bobbing in a churn of white water. The pirates all gave a ragged cheer. The chasing ships, which could just be seen as dark, star-blocking hulks, started to slip beneath the horizon.

Rip, who was spying from a hidey-hole, sensed the Bigs unwind a bit. Runa and Abel yawned but they were happier.

This was not such good news for the rats: from now on the Bigs would have more time to notice what was going on under their noses and feet.

# Chapter 9: The Long Way Round

'Where are we going now?' said Runa to Abel when he clambered down the rigging and dropped to the deck.

'Captain Blanche is setting course for Japan,' said Abel. 'It is far west from here.' He turned his back to the rising sun and pointed.

'But that's the wrong way,' said Runa, despairing. 'I'll never reach Sweden again. And I miss my white ratty.'

Abel held her hand and squeezed it.

'I'm sorry,' she said, gulping back her sorrow. 'Never mind me. You don't even know where your home is and you must miss your whole family. I should be brave, like you. I'm sure when we reach Japan we will meet with the *Hydromyst* — I mean, the *Black Caesar* — again. Then I'll see my ratty. Then, surely, I will find a way home.'

It was a long voyage with some hair-raising moments. Several times, Abel spotted shark fins trailing behind the ship after the cook threw a bowl of bloody slops into the sea. Once, the captain asked five of her men to take the jollyboat up the mouth of a river to scout for good, fresh water and they were driven off by a group of forest warriors who were understandably not keen to see strangers from who-knows-where. Three days later, on the open sea, Runa spotted a bird with wings so wide she thought for a moment it was a dragon.

Abel and Runa became very good friends. She taught him hop-scotch, pat-a-cake and all the games he had never been allowed to play and, in return, he taught her the songs he remembered.

But while the small Bigs got a taste of how thrilling pirate life could be, and how lovely a good friendship is, a drama was unfolding right under their noses.

Rip struggled to keep the rats strictly in line.

As the ship sailed down the coast of South America, she found herself dashing all over the deck to sort out fights and keep everyone hidden and safe.

Any time there was an argument, a rat set off to fetch her. Rip listened to both sides and, most often, she split the fighting rats up to calm down. Sometimes she had to sit on them if they were particularly angry.

She even made sure the rats changed their toilet habits. Instead of pooping everywhere, she told them to drop their waste in the bilges. That way the Bigs wouldn't see rat mess everywhere and get suspicious. They were also careful about food. Rip got Patch and Peg to share their rations, so the plates were licked clean each night. Not a crumb was left. And she made sure the only barrels and sacks nibbled and raided were stacked out of sight.

Not everyone was grateful.

'The Bigs have not hurt us yet,' said Spite, to anyone who would listen. 'Why should we live like this?'

Slink said: 'Yes, she's right. We should have all the food we want, not these small crumbs.'

'I think that too,' said Sharp.

'Me too,' said Twitch, with a nervous tremble of his head.

After a week of trying to be everywhere all the time, Rip spoke to Patch and Peg.

She said: 'You've got to help. I can't do all this. You know the ship best of all.'

'We do!' said Peg, with pride.

'So I will put you in charge of some things. You can show rats where it is safe to chew on things and where to make nests. Patch, I want you to help keep the peace.'

'Aye-aye,' said Patch.

But even then, the rats still pestered Rip for advice or simply to moan about the strict rules.

When it all got too much, Rip found Abel.

The boy was different from the Bigs she'd met before. He was still and quiet so he didn't scare her. He knew about the rats so there was no point hiding from him. Best of all, unlike Runa who couldn't resist trying to stroke her, he never tried to touch Rip.

She sat next to him in the basket and chirped: 'You are not so bad for a Big,' but he didn't understand.

Rip did not know it yet, but slowly, Abel was getting over his fear of rats – and it was all because of her. She sat still and did not dart about. She became a familiar face. Best of all, she had no interest in climbing onto him or biting him.

'You are not so bad for a rat,' he said, but she didn't understand.

The *Liberté* sailed south, past the Tropic of Capricorn, down and further down and then around Cape Horn. This was a notoriously treacherous part of the sea which claimed the lives of many sailors. The passages were narrow with high waves, strong currents and savage storms.

One day, there was a moment that sent a chill down everyone's spines. Rip noticed it as she sat lookout with Abel. She stood on the edge of the basket. The rat wrinkled her nose and sniffed, sniffed and sniffed at something unknown. It smelled like water, winter and danger. She stretched out and Abel had to put his hand out to make sure she didn't topple over and fall.

'What's out there, Rat?' he asked.

Then he saw the gigantic iceberg.

Abel hollered down to the crew and soon all hands were on deck. Half of them helping to navigate the unexpected ice-floe, armed with long sticks to push off any smaller icebergs that floated too near. The other half, which included Runa, gaped at the bobbing ice. None of them had seen anything like it before.

One wrong turn and the ship might have crashed into the ice. Captain Blanche kept her nerve and a strong hand on the wheel.

Thanks to Rip, the *Liberté* cruised through without disaster.

Once free of the ice, Captain Blanche turned the ship to a different bearing, pushing out into the vastness of the Pacific Ocean.

The islands dotting this part of the world were not well charted. Explorers were still exploring, map-makers were still map-making and the inhabitants of the islands were still not used to people from the other side of the world poking around their homes.

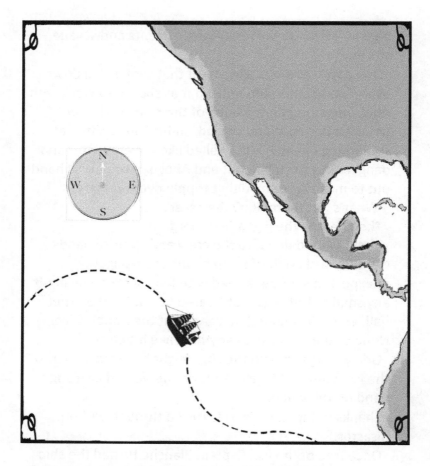

So the voyages of the *Liberté*, and the *Black Caesar* before it, were fraught with risk.

But the gamble was paying off.

It took them more than a month to sail down to the Cape, then they sailed north for another month and a half, riding the wind and currents.

Then Rip had a particularly stressful day.

All the rats who liked her, or at least wanted to be in her good books, were trying to cosy up to her. One way rats show their trust in each other is to sleep together in a big pile.

Rip's pile was almost too big to manage. Day or night, any time she settled down for a nap in her hammock, she would find five or six other rats trying to climb in with her. They lay on top and sometimes there was barely room for her to poke her nose out from under someone's belly to breathe.

Unfortunately, rats also like to gnaw. Her guests could not help nibbling at the cloth.

That morning, the fraying hammock finally gave way under the weight of the snoozing rats and snapped, dumping them on to the floor. Most of them tumbled on top of Rip. This was not a good way to wake up.

Rip pulled herself out of the heap of wriggling rats.

'Oh, you are such a *pain*!' she told them all.

'Oops,' said one.

'Get lost, the lot of you!' said Rip.

'We just want to be friends,' said another.

'Go.'

They went, but their ears were high with unhappiness and their tails drooped with dejection.

'You should be nice to them,' said Gold. 'You need to stay on their good side or you will lose them.'

'I don't care,' said Rip. 'I'm fed up.'

But Gold was right. Trouble was brewing, and more and more rats were listening to Spite, Sharp and their whispers.

'There is no room,' Rip heard the rats moan.

'Where do you go when I need you?' grumbled another.

'I need a break, you know,' said Rip, but she felt guilty about running off to find Abel.

Then disaster struck.

# Chapter 10: Drought and Spite

At first, no one noticed it hadn't rained for a while. It was very warm and the rats spent a lot of time lying around in the shade trying to keep cool.

But the sun beat down on the *Liberté*. The water level in the bilges sank until they were nearly dry. The sky was cloudless. There were no puddles to lap from or buckets to plunge into.

The sun started bleaching the wood and scorching people's skin, and Captain Blanche ordered the crew to halve their drink rations. The rats started to worry.

'Rip, we need to drink.'

'Where can we go to drink?'

'I have such a thirst!'

Rip did not know what to say.

'I need a think,' she told them.

What could one little rat do about a drought?

She went to find Abel as she could plan better when she was left alone by the other rats. The warmth made her feel heavy and sleepy. Rip was from a cold climate. She did not like the Tropics.

'This is bad,' she said to Abel. 'If my rats can't drink then they will die. I don't know what to do.'

But her voice was so high-pitched the Big couldn't hear it – and he wouldn't have understood her anyway.

Rip still had no idea by the time she came down.

A circle of rats waited for her, lying like furry puddles in the shade. They spread their tails and bodies to lose as much heat as possible. They all looked at her with hope in their eyes.

'What should we do?' said Patch.

'I don't have a plan,' Rip had to say.

The rats started meeping and peeping in alarm.

'Please keep calm,' said Rip, but it did not work.

She was as unhappy as the others. Her tongue was dry, her fur felt dusty and her brain was hot and bothered. The only fresh water she could think of was kept in casks in the hold. These were made of thick, seasoned wood which would take ages to gnaw through - except for a hole in the side which was plugged with cork. This cork was soft but it was too high for a rat to reach.

Rip felt hopeless as she pattered back to Captain Blanche's cabin for a snooze.

'Ugh,' she said when she saw the hammock hanging from one end, the other trailing on the deck. She remembered climbing up and out of the pile of rats... and an idea struck.

She had a plan.

'I need you three to come with me,' said Rip to Patch, Peg and Gold. 'I know how to get us a drink.'

Rip led her little team down to the hold and found a cask of water.

'What do we do?' said Peg.

'You and Patch stand close. Gold, I want you to get on top of them. Then I will try to climb up you and grab the cork – watch out, there will be a big splash when I get it out!'

'Good work,' said Patch.

The boys braced themselves and Gold stood on them, his front paws on Peg's back and his feet on Patch's shoulders. Then Rip scrambled up, holding their fur.

'Ouch-ouch,' said Gold.

They made an unsteady pyramid. Rip teetered on the top and pressed against the side of the cask. She could just touch the cork with her nose.

'I need more height!' she said.

'Right,' said Peg. He and Patch stood on tip-toes. Gold arched his back. Rip stretched.

'I gock ick,' she said, burying her teeth in the cork. She tried to pull but that made the rats below squeak and wobble.

'Rip it, Rip!' said Peg.

Rip attacked the stopper with her teeth. Bits of cork flew in every direction. She used her sharp incisors to hollow out the whole thing. Soon, she could push her whole head inside. The water was so close – she could smell it. Rip pulled back.

'It won't be long now,' she said. 'When I chew through, it will spill out fast. Just drop me and call all the rats to come down here and lap it up quick.'

'Yes, boss,' said Patch.

Rip went back to business on the cork, but before she could breach the cask, she felt Gold give way beneath her.

'Eek!' she went as she fell.

She was furious with her friends. They let her down.
Then she saw why.

Patch, Peg and Gold were pinned to the floor by other
rats. Rip recognised Sharp, Slink and Sneak. Twitch was
running nervously back and forth. Spite was standing in
the middle looking very smug.

'Let them go,' said Rip.

'No, I don't think we will,' said Spite.

'Let me back up there,' said Rip. 'We can all have a
drink. It will save us.'

'We don't need you,' said Spite. 'You aren't one of us.

'I don't think she saved us last time,' said another rat
called Stink. 'Things have been bad since you brought us
on to this ship. We want to eat when and where we like.
We don't want you to tell us what to do.'

'Yeah, you tricked us,' said Sharp.

Rip tried to keep her temper.

'Why would I do that?' she said, grating her teeth.

'You got to be the boss-rat,' sneered Spite.

Rip puffed all her fur up.

'I did not *want* to be boss rat. I did not *ask* to be boss
rat. I just do my best.'

'Then you will not mind if we take the job off you,' said
Spite.

Rip realised what was happening. This was mutiny!

# Chapter 11: Outcast

Rip squatted down and prepared to fight.

'Back down,' said Spite. 'Your friends can't help. There are more of us than you.'

'What will you do if I don't give up?' said Rip.

'We will hurt them,' said Spite. To prove they weren't bluffing, Sharp bit Patch, tearing his ear. The young rat squealed.

Rip's ears shot up.

'Stop that,' she said.

'We will let your friends go if they give up on you and join us,' said Spite.

'Rip is our friend,' said Peg, but his voice went muffled when Sneak sat on his head.

Gold struggled, but Stink, Slink and Swipe held him down.

If she ran, Rip hoped, they might chase her and leave her friends alone. But for now she was surrounded.

'You see,' said Spite. 'We don't like how you do things. You tell us to hide from the Bigs, but then you spend time with one.'

'It was how I got some peace,' said Rip.

'I don't care,' said Spite. 'We don't know who you are or where you come from and we don't trust you. We will go our own way. There will be no rules.'

'Yeah,' said Stink.

'There were rats here once. You can still smell their trails, like ghost-scents,' said Rip. 'Where do you think they went? If there are no rules, then the Bigs will kill us.'

'No!' screamed Spite. 'I saw the way Bigs rule Bigs. I saw them in chains on our old ship. I saw them get hurt. I saw them stuck in the cage. They did not get to choose where to go or when to eat.

'We are rats. We do not need to be like Bigs with their bad rules. No Skip, no boss rat. We will all do what we want. We will all be free.'

Rip did not know how to say that true freedom did not mean the end of all rules. She knew what it was like to live beneath a tyrant who made up his own cruel law. But some rules made sense.

'Just let me get us a drink,' said Rip. 'We can be friends...'

'No one will be your friend,' said Spite. 'You are cast out. You have no friends here. Not one. If a rat speaks to you then we will cast them out, too.'

This was a dreadful threat. There are few things more important to rats than friends and family.

Spite continued, 'If we see you, we will fight you. There are eight of us and one of you. Who do you think will win?'

Rip hissed a dreadful rat swearword. It made Spite flinch.

This gave Rip the chance to dive past the gang of rats. She skittered up to where the pirates relaxed in their hammocks. She ran along the edge of one like a tightrope and jumped to the next.

The eight rats followed on behind, creeping with their flanks to the walls. Rip did not dare drop down to the floor.

She found Abel's hammock. Very carefully, she flattened down small, careful not to touch his bare feet.

Spite and her friends prowled around, frustrated.

'You stay up there!' shouted Spite. 'Or we'll get you.'

'Yeah, be friends with a Big,' said Swipe. 'See how that works for you.'

'You are a lone rat now, Rip,' said Spite. 'Don't speak to your friends or we will hurt them. You can't sniff-sniff or sleep in a rat pile. If you do, we will find you – and you don't want that.'

Rip shivered.

The other rats stalked away.

She licked her paws and cleaned her face to calm down. Though Rip was a rat who enjoyed peace and quiet, she still needed friends. Some rare rats are natural loners but Rip was not one of them. She already felt abandoned.

Rats left on their own too long become sad, sorry creatures.

Rip wished she had Lu and Preen with her. She missed cuddling up with her Mum Rat.

She fell asleep, snuffling unhappily to herself.

Abel woke her when he rolled over and slid out of the hammock. Rip fell out too. Instantly, she remembered the horrible events of the day before.

'Psst,' she heard. She turned about. 'Psst!'

The sound was coming from Peg. He was well hidden behind a wooden chest. Patch and Gold were there too.

'Hi,' said Rip. Hope flared in her. 'Do you still like me?'

'Yes,' said Gold.

'We don't want you to be a lone rat,' said Peg, in a whisper. He smelled anxious.

'But...' said Rip.

'But there are only three of us,' said Patch, 'and lots of them.'

'I know,' said Rip. 'It would be best if you don't come near me from now on.'

'Rip...' said Peg, apologetically. 'We don't like this.'

'I know,' said Rip. 'Go on.'

'We will see you when we can,' promised Patch, as he and his brother turned tail.

'Well,' said Gold, sadly. 'At least you get your wish. I will have to leave you be.'

'This is not what I meant,' said Rip, her whiskers drooping, but they'd already gone.

It rained solidly for six days and the pirates rolled out all the empty barrels to catch the falling water. Rip was glad no one had to worry about thirst, but she felt unsafe on her own. Sharp eyes watched her as she went around the ship. Abel made her feel more secure so she spent a lot of time pattering around after him. The young pirate got so used to her he started looking around to make sure she was near. He noticed she looked a bit worse for wear. Rats help wash each other, especially difficult to reach places– but of course Rip had no one to do that. She also felt tired, lonely and less bothered about her fur. Her eyes and nose were rimmed with red. This was a sign of how unhappy she was.

'You are turning into a scruff,' said Abel. 'You are a bit ratty, Rat.'

Though she felt forlorn, Rip noticed things were going wrong for the rats on the *Black Caesar*.

At first it was fun. The rats feasted and ran riot. One morning, they woke to find all the food containers thoroughly sealed. Of course, rats being rats, it didn't take long for them to find another way in, but this did not bode well. Next, a Big plugged a few rat runs with wads of cloth. A few moments of biting and clawing got them loose but still Rip worried.

With Spite, Slink and the others in charge, the rats stopped being so careful. They fought a lot. Once or twice Rip smelled blood.

Then a bored sailor fired his pistol at a rat who unwisely decided to run across a busy deck in daylight. It was Twitch. He escaped with just a fright but when Rip heard the *bang!* and the shocked squeak, she felt surer than ever the rats should keep to the shadows.

# Chapter 12: War is Declared

The pirates called a council, which Abel and Runa went to, sitting cross-legged at the front of the crowd.

A burly buccaneer raised his hand and Captain Blanche said, 'Yes?'

'Ma'am, there are more rats aboard. They have chewed my clothes to tatters and put droppings all over the galley. Begging your pardon, captain, as I know you have a liking for your two pets, but I think we have an infestation.'

'Aye,' said another. 'I heard them squeaking and scratching about these last few nights.'

'We haven't made landfall for weeks,' said Captain Blanche. 'It's strange this has only become a problem now.'

'Our food will only last so long,' said the quartermaster.

'I know,' sighed Captain Blanche. 'I love my two boys but my crew must come first. What do you propose?'

'A bounty on every five tails,' said the Bosun.

'We have no poison or traps.'

'Traps can be made.'

'No,' whispered Runa to Abel. 'Don't let them.'

'We put it to the vote,' said Captain Blanche. 'All in favour raise your right hand- if you have one. Runa, as a hostage, you have no vote.'

Every pirate put their hand up, apart from those who raised stumps or hooks. Everyone except Abel.

'I would have thought you would be the first to say aye,' said Captain Blanche. 'You have no love for rats.'

'Some of them aren't so bad,' said Abel, quietly.

'Still, the motion is carried,' said the Captain. She did not sound happy. 'Begin making the traps. Just – try not to catch or hurt my boys.'

The first clue Rip had that something changed was when Runa tried to drop a box over her. Rip was too fast. She escaped just as it touched her tail. The girl tried to grab her but Rip leaped out of the way and vanished beneath a bunk.

'If only we could tell her we want to catch her to keep her safe,' said Runa. She knelt down and tried to scoop Rip out, but Rip's teeth flashed and Runa yelped.

'We'll just have to hope she is clever enough not to get caught,' said Abel.

Rip watched suspiciously at the Bigs working with pieces of wood, bent wire and string. Their creation reminded her of the box Runa tried to trap her in.

Though the other rats grew braver, playing out in the open and knocking things over, none of them came close to Rip.

'Hey,' she whispered to one rat. 'Hey, you. Tell your friends to watch out and use their wits. The Bigs have made a strange box. Keep far from it or you will get caught.'

But the rat did not touch noses, speak to her or even look at her. She felt like a ghost.

On the day the pirates were ready to set the trap, Rip sat in the rigging next to Abel and Runa. They were splicing ropes, a job which called for small, clever fingers.

'What do you want to do?' said Runa to Abel. 'When you grow up, I mean.'

'Live,' said Abel, 'and be free.'

'I know that,' said Runa. 'But you can't be a pirate all your life, especially these days. What do you want to be, one day?'

'I would like to sail,' said Abel. 'I would like to have my own ship and take it where I wanted. I will live on the sea all my life. And I will sing as I sail. I worry sometimes I will forget my own songs, and when that happens I will forget everything about my home and family, too. But if I find someone else who knows my songs then perhaps I can follow the music home.'

'Or you could live with me,' said Runa, 'And make a new home. But that's up to you.'

'What about you, Runa?'

'Oh, I want to learn. Not needlework and how to wear nice dresses, like my Pappa wants me to do. I want to learn all I can about animals and draw them. I would teach people about rats, of course, but also about birds and lizards and bats – all the things I've seen so far. Maybe if you get your ship we can chart a voyage to explore the world and find new species.'

They heard clattering below.

'Runa,' said Abel, his face suddenly serious. 'They've put the traps out.'

# Chapter 13: The Traps

Rip slid down the ropes as fast as she could go.

'Don't go near the new box,' she cheeped, but no one would listen. The rats just turned aside and hurried away. Then Stink saw her.

'You should not be down here,' he said.

'Stink, you must watch out,' said Rip. 'The Bigs have made this thing and it can't be good.'

'Why?' said Stink. 'What does it do?'

'I – I don't know,' said Rip. 'But a Big tried to trap me in a box like this.'

But Stink was not paying attention.

'Spite!' he shouted. 'Sneak, come quick. The out-cast has tried to speak to us. She broke our rules.'

'Get her!' said Sneak.

Rip fled.

That night, while the lamps shone puddles of light on the weather deck, Rip watched from above as the rats came out.

Some were very hungry. Others tussled and played. Rip stayed out of sight, up in the rigging.

She watched one rat, then another, inspect the strange box. It was baited with tasty bits of fish. The temptation was too much for one of the ship rats and he stepped inside. The wire twanged and the box snapped shut. The rat was trapped.

His friends patted at the side of the box, probing for a weakness. There was none. The panicked prisoner gnawed and scrabbled but there was no way out.

Rip waited until the other rats gave up. Then she dropped from the rigging and went over to the box.

'Hi,' she said to the other rat. 'I am here to help.'

'Please let me out,' said the trapped rat. It was Shriek, one of Spite's friends. Suddenly he didn't care Rip was an outcast.

'I will try,' said Rip.

She sniffed all round the box. It was well-built and the spring that held the door shut did not yield to her teeth.

'Why are you here?' said Shriek, in a very small voice. 'You don't like me.'

'*Kree*,' said Rip, simply. She pulled at the door with her paws but it didn't budge. She started to gnaw at the wood. It splintered in her mouth.

'Thank you,' said Shriek. 'Please work fast.'

Rip kept nibbling as hard as she could, but the wood was thick. She didn't have time. The sun was coming up. There were loud footsteps. Rip looked up. A sailor loomed over the trap, his face a picture of disgust.

'Get away,' he kicked at Rip and, when that didn't work, he lifted his foot to stamp on her.

'Run, Rip!' shouted Shriek. She had no choice.

When Rip came back to check, the trap was empty and reset.

Upset, Rip ran along the outside railing, sure-footed though the ship was rocking in the waves, and she jumped up to the prow. A long bowsprit – a bit like a horizontal mast – jutted out from the front of the ship. Rip ran along it until she reached the end. There was someone behind her. She turned.

To her surprise, it was tiny Twitch. He was never still. His head moved in little jerking motions and his eyes swivelled this way and that.

'I don't want to hurt you,' said Rip, 'but I could. I am twice your size.'

'You don't have to,' said Twitch. Then, astonishingly, he sniff-sniffed with her. 'I can't stay long. I just want to say not all the rats think Spite is right. They don't think this is fair.'

'Is this true?' said Rip.

'Yes. Your friends are still on your side. They speak for you. That's why you are left in peace. Spite knows if they hurt you the other rats might not like it.'

'This is a trick,' said Rip.

Twitch twitched.

'It's not,' he said. 'I saw you try to help Shriek. You are a good rat. Look, I have to go or Spite will know we talked.'

'Will the rats fight for me if I strike first?' said Rip.

'No, but nor will they fight for Spite if she strikes first.'

'Hmm,' said Rip. 'Thank you.'

'Bye.'

Rip was not sure she trusted the jumpy little runt. It could be Spite was trying to lure her out. But if he was telling the truth, then all she had to do was get rid of the ringleader rats.

The new danger did not send the rats back into hiding. Either Spite, Sneak and the rest of them didn't understand what the traps were or they didn't care. The feasting and fighting continued.

Two more traps appeared.

Three more rats vanished that night.

Rip stared at the boxes. She hoped Patch, Peg and Gold were safe. She sat back on her haunches and brushed her whiskers. There had to be something she could do.

# Chapter 14: Marooned

Abel called from the top of the mast.

'Land ho!'

Rip followed Abel like a little shadow as he helped attach the jollyboat to the pulley and arm, ready to lower it into the sea.

The *Liberté* set anchor in water so blue it put the sky to shame. The pirates worked with fevered excitement. They drew lots to see who would go ashore first. Abel and Runa both won.

Rip looked at the jollyboat and narrowed her eyes. She remembered being scooped up in a hat and placed on a wooden bench. This floating wood thing brought her to the ship.

She sniffed deeply. The scents of hot sand and foliage came to her. She remembered watching Black Spot skulk off the ship. If only Spite's gang would do that – but why would they when they had the power?

A plan formed.

She sped off down to the hold. Rats scattered away from her but she didn't care. She squeaked and stamped her feet as loud as she could.

'Hey,' she said. 'Hey, all of you! The ship has stopped.'

'Shh Rip,' said Twitch. 'We can hear you.'

'Good! Come and hear me, rats!'

Sure enough, Spite appeared. She waited until Sneak, Stink and the rest of her gang were there.

'Are you mad or thick, Rip?' she said. 'You should not be here. You are cast out.'

'So what?' said Rip. 'I might be a lone rat but I am a pi-rat too. Pi-rats do as they please. Do you know what I want to do?'

'No...' said Spite.

'This!'

And Rip turned round and slapped Spite in the face with her tail and piddled right under Sharp's nose.

'Right, that's it. Get her!' shrieked Spite.

The gang went for Rip. She turned and ran.

She was not the fastest rat. They would catch her before long, but she didn't need long for her plan to work.

She led them outside.

She was just in time. The jollyboat was lifting from the deck.

Rip leaped, caught the top with her front paws. She used her back legs to kick herself over and in. Spite and three of her cronies flew after her like high-jumpers. They were so angry they didn't care about the Bigs.

The pirates heaved on the rope and the boat swung over the side of the ship. The pulleys squeaked as the Bigs started to winch it down to the waves.

The boat shook as Runa and the pirates climbed in.

Rip hid between Abel's ankles.

Spite's ears were high with rage.

'You... you...'

The pirates worked the oars. It took a few minutes to row to the beach. Abel hopped over the side, not caring the sea soaked his trousers. He helped pull the boat up the sand. Runa jumped out too, laughing with joy when she felt firm land beneath her feet.

Rip was the first rat to scramble out of the boat.

She smelled greenery and fresh water.

'What... what is this?' Spite clambered around on the sand. She walked oddly, tipping from one side to the other.

'I feel ill,' said Stink. 'Bleurgh, ick.' But though he made strange noises, he could not be sick.

Rip realised everyone had spent so long on a floating ship it felt weird to be on solid ground.

She staggered a bit. The sand felt strange too. She was used to her claws click-tapping on wood. Now she moved quietly, the grains shifting between her toes.

'Where did you take us, out-cast?' hissed Spite. 'What did you do?'

'I said the ship was too full,' said Rip. 'I thought it would be good to leave it for a bit.'

'Come back to the boat,' Spite said to Stink, Slink and Sharp.

If they got back into the jollyboat, Rip might lose her chance to keep them off the *Black Caesar*. Already, two of the pirates were digging their feet into the sand to push the boat back out and pick up their next passengers.

'Hey, you lot,' she said. 'Fight me, right here, right now.'

'You are mad, Rip,' said Stink. 'There are four of us. You are on your own. We will tear you to bits.'

Rip hadn't had a real battle for a very long time, not since she had beaten Thug, a rat who looked fierce but had a soft heart beneath the muscle. This was different. Four rats were far more dangerous than one. Never in her whole life had Rip deliberately picked a fight.

'I can take you on. I'm not scared,' she lied.

If she could keep them talking long enough, the boat would pull away and she could stop them going back to the *Liberté*.

But Spite and the others weren't going to waste time. They were full of hate and it exploded out of them in a whirl of claws and teeth.

Rip was surrounded.

She scratched and snapped but the gang piled onto her. They tore at her fur, pulled her tail and pushed her into the sand.

Rip scrabbled to stand up, but they wouldn't let her. She rolled onto her back. This exposed her soft belly but it meant she could use all four paws and her fearsome jaws.

Still, it was not enough. Slink and Stink held her down and she wriggled as Spite laughed.

'*Kree!*' Rip shouted. 'I give up. *Kree!*'

But Spite, Stink, Slink and Sharp were mad with malicious joy. Finally, they had an excuse to hurt Rip and there was no reason to stop.

'There is no *kree*,' Spite giggled.

Rip kicked out to push Sharp away but Slink caught her foot in his mouth. Sharp's teeth were in her tail.

They made terrible noises. Even to a rat, the sounds weren't close to words any more. They shrieked and laughed and squealed.

She couldn't hold them all off...

None of them heard the *scrunch-boom, scrunch-boom* of huge feet approaching.

Then a sheet of cold water fell on them, drenching them all. Slink and her gang leaped away, bedraggled and shocked.

Rip, still on her back, looked into the gaping mouth of a bailing bucket. Beyond that, she saw strong brown hands – Big hands – and even further up, blurry with distance, was Abel's face.

'Go on, shoo- shoo,' said Runa, kicking sand at the angry, wet rats.

Rip flipped over and shook herself like a dog. She looked up the beach and saw Spite running away toward a dense pocket of undergrowth. Slink and the others were racing to get away from the Bigs, too. Stink fled across the beach, his bottom going up and down as he bounded away. Sharp dived into a rockpool.

Rip didn't stop to say 'thank you' to her saviours. She turned and sprinted back to the jollyboat. It was now afloat and two pirates were standing up to their thighs in the surf, pushing it further out. She felt battered, bruised and beaten, but Rip made one last, arching jump into the little craft.

She sat, shivering in a puddle in the foot-well until the boat moved off. Then she risked peering over the stern.

The four rats collected their wits and reached the sea
but none of them wanted to go into the bubbling water.
 'Kree, Spite!' shouted Rip, from where she sat,
watching the distance between them grow.

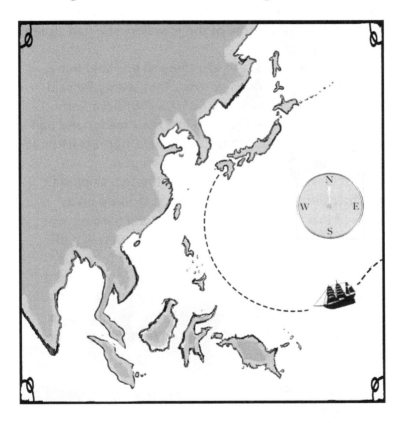

# Chapter 15: Old Friends

From there on, the voyage to Japan was easier for the Bigs. They landed on islands where people traded with them. For every basket of food, Captain Blanche insisted on leaving a gift of some of the jewellery she had stolen from the *Amitié*.

'That's not a very pirate-like thing to do,' said Runa.

Abel shrugged. 'Pirates do what they want,' he said.

Things were easier for the rats, too. Without Spite, Slink and the others, the gang lost their leader and half their squad. Rip was the Skip and the other rats listened to her again. Now the traps stayed empty.

At last, several long months after the two ships split up, the *Liberté* and the *Black Caesar* moored up as planned in a sheltered cove. The natural harbour was surrounded by jagged cliffs. Elegant trees grew with slim, knotty trunks. This was the island of Tokudaia.

A great cheer went up as soon as the pirates turned the bend and spotted the *Black Caesar* at anchor. A second round of cheers erupted from the other ship.

Captain Blanche ordered her men to row over at once.

Runa begged to go across too.

'I need to see my ratty.'

'And see her you shall,' said the Captain, her eyes ablaze with joy.

Of course it was not that simple. It was a long time since Runa had seen her little friend. Anything could have happened.

Rip, who smelled the familiar bulk of the fat *fluyt* now known as the *Black Caesar*, was worried, too. The last time she'd spoken to Lu, they'd argued. Lu told her off for biting Runa. Were they still friends?

Rip sat on Abel's knee as the pirates rowed the jollyboat. She was very nervous. Her eyes were wide and goggling.

The boat drew closer and closer until the hull of the *Black Caesar* filled her world.

The pirates climbed aboard and Rip went too, clutching Abel's trouser leg. She plopped onto the weather deck and went in search of her sisters as the two captains embraced, Blanche giving Rouge a long kiss.

Rip picked up a scent and followed it to the galley, squeezing herself flat to get under the door.

Yes, Preen and Lu had been here, for sure, but they weren't there now.

Rip waddled down to the lower decks.

They were not on the orlop, though one familiar rat was. Rip smelled him long before she saw him.

'Pew!' she said.

'Young Rip,' said Pew. 'Long time no see. How are ye?' They sniff-sniffed.

'Fine, thanks. How are you?'

'Oh,' he said, shifting arthritically. 'I be all aches and pains but good, but for that. You be on the look out for white rat and grey rat?'

'Yes,' said Rip, excited.

'They ain't here no more.'

Rip let out a squeak of despair.

'No,' she said. 'Oh, no.'

'I'd look high up if I were you,' said Pew with a wink.

Rip did not know what to make of this, but she went upstairs and back onto the outside deck. She had forgotten how much bigger this ship was. The spaces felt wide open and there was more to search.

She came to the captain's cabin.

Rouge walked toward the closed door with Captain Blanche beside her.

'I saved the very best vintage for when we met again,' said Rouge as she pushed the door open. 'Now is the time to open it, I think!'

'I agree,' said Captain Blanche, warmly.

Rip grabbed the opportunity to dash through the doorway before it shut.

The pirate captains poured out something strong and red and clinked glasses, laughing all the while.

'To our freedom!' said Captain Blanche.

'To us,' said Captain Rouge.

Rip paid no notice. She scuttled around and found a scent – it was Preen and the trail led to a cupboard. She climbed the carved wood and scratched her way to the top.

There were two bowls, one full of water, one full of scraps of fish and fruit. There was a hammock and inside it were two loosely stuffed pillows. The green one was fat and lumpy, the red one was ripped and torn.

Rip could smell rats but she could not see them. She climbed onto the green pillow to have a look. One of the lumps squeaked. A grey nose pointed through a hole in the fabric. Rip touched her own nose to it curiously.

'Preen?' she said.

'Rip?'

Preen struggled free. All Rip's worries vanished when she saw her sister.

'Who is it?' said another lump.

A pink nose emerged followed by a white rat.

'Lu!'

They sniffed each other all over.

'I'm so glad to smell you,' said Lu.

'I'm glad to smell you, too,' said Rip.

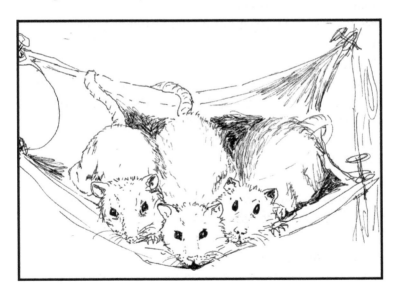

'I let them in here because they reminded me of your boys,' said Captain Rouge.

'The white one is special to the girl,' said Captain Blanche. 'We should bring her over.'

Runa was delighted to be reunited with Lu and Preen. She played with them for hours.

But after a while, a nagging feeling stole over her.

'Abel,' she said, as they sat on the deck with their feet sole-to-sole. The rats leaped over their legs to play.

'Yes?'

'Where are the rest of the crew? The old crew, I mean. What happened to them? Did the pirates throw them overboard or strand them on a desert island? Did they make them walk the plank?'

'Pirates don't really do that,' said Abel. 'The plank, I mean.'

'Oh, phew,' said Runa.

'They do keel-haul people, instead,' said Abel. 'That's when someone is put in ropes and dragged under the ship. They pull what's left up the other side.'

'Yuck,' said Runa, horrified. 'Have your crew ever done that?'

'Er,' said Abel.

'Anyway, I want to go to the brig and see if my old captain is still there,' said Runa.

'I don't think Captain Blanche...'

'Captain Rouge and Captain Blanche are too busy with each other to notice. They won't know.' Runa set her lips. 'Come with me or don't. It's up to you.'

'Oh, all right then,' said Abel.

They waited until the two Captains sailed off in the *Liberté* on some mysterious mission. Then they crept to the brig, carefully - because neither of them wanted to explain what they were doing if they were spotted by a curious pirate.

The brig door had a hatch which opened from the outside. Runa flipped it and she peered through.

A very pale face looked back.

'Runa,' said the Dutch Captain. 'You're alive. Thank goodness. You have to free us. We're dying in here.'

# Chapter 16: Dejima

Runa knew the door wouldn't budge. It was soundly locked.

Curious, Abel looked at the imprisoned crew.

The Captain flinched.

'It's another of those pirate devils!'

'This is Abel,' said Runa, in Dutch. 'He isn't a devil. He's my friend. He helped me.'

'Did you help the girl?' the Captain asked Abel.

'Yes,' said Runa quickly before Abel could open his mouth. 'But he doesn't speak Dutch. I've been kept for ransom but Abel helps me sneak out. He might have to lock me up again in a bit, though,' she whispered.

'Oh, I do apologise, young sir,' said the Captain. 'It has been so long since we have seen a friendly face.'

'Are you hurt?'

'We have not been used ill. They gave us food and water. But I fear we are weak from lack of light, good air and exercise. My men are on the verge of scurvy.'

To show what he meant, one of the sailors prodded a tooth which wobbled alarmingly. Another could barely stand.

'I'll find a way to get you out of here,' said Runa. 'I promise.'

They heard footsteps.

'We have to go,' said Abel and he slammed the hatch with one hand and grabbed Runa's arm with the other.

Runa was lost in thought for most of the day. She could not see a way of freeing the sailors. She had no idea where the key to the brig was kept, nor how to pinch it.

'It's a shame they don't understand us,' she said to Abel as they watched the rats play. 'We could tell them to find and bring us the key. But I suppose this is not a fairy tale.'

'What would happen if you freed them?' said Abel. 'You would have a bunch of weak, thin men with no weapons staggering about. We – the pirates I mean – would catch them in seconds.'

'You're right,' sighed Runa.

The next day the *Liberté* came sailing back into sight.

Captain Blanche boarded the *Black Caesar* waving a piece of paper triumphantly.

'We caught a trader on their way out of port,' she said. 'All we have to do is make a copy of the paper and we shall have our booty! Runa, I will need your sharp eyes, my dear. Come to the captain's quarters at four bells.'

'Yes ma'am.'

She found Blanche leaning over the desk with several quills and pots of ink by her hand. Rip was sitting in a hammock.

'I asked you here because of all my crew, you are the only one who can read,' said the Captain. 'I don't expect you to know Japanese but you can at least make sure the Dutch is acceptable.'

'Aye Captain,' said Runa. She wondered if now was the time to bargain for the Dutch crew.

The pirate worked away for a while, carefully selecting nibs and ink. Sometimes the quill scratched on the paper but most of the time the captain sat poised, studying the papers she was copying. Now and then, when the ink was drying, she beckoned Runa to look at it.

'It seems fine,' said Runa.

'I expect,' said Captain Blanche, 'you are wondering how I can read and write?'

'No ma'am,' said Runa. 'Well, I am now, I suppose.'

'My master was a man of many passions, including calligraphy and cartography. That is, writing and maps. He taught me for a bet. His friends wagered a half-African girl would not have the brains to learn. My master won the bet.' She picked up the knife to sharpen a new quill. 'When he went blind, I read to him. He liked me to describe books on navigation and the charts of the sea and sky.'

Runa looked at the knife. She'd played at being a pirate for months without really thinking about what it meant. It had all been an adventure to her. But seeing her old captain in the hold, miserable and sick, made her feel differently. Had Captain Blanche killed people just for that piece of paper?

'We all have our talents,' said Captain Blanche. 'We have to learn. It enables us to survive. And my men have survived a lot.' She scattered sand on the paper to dry the ink and blew it off. 'With this bounty, we may be able to begin new lives. Free lives. It looks perfect. What do you think, Runa?'

'Perfect,' the girl whispered, wondering if she really was just a hostage after all.

'I will gather my men. The sailors who joined us from the *Black Caesar* will make a good escort. One of them will have to speak for me, of course. They are unlikely to suspect us of piracy if we bring an innocent little blonde child to shore. I think you would make a convincing Dutch girl. What do you think? Would you like to visit Japan?'

Runa nodded uncertainly.

'Then it is settled. I will call for you.'

Runa looked at the spare sheets of paper. Perhaps she could make use of them somehow.

'May I have some of that?' she said. 'I should like to draw my white ratty and any animals I see on Japan.'

'Of course. Take a pencil also,' said Captain Blanche.

Runa tucked the sheaf of paper under her arm and hurried off.

Rip got up, stretched and yawned. She climbed down and left the cabin. There was a lot of to-ing and fro-ing. Sailors shuttled back and forth between the barque and the *fluyt*. Captain Blanche wanted a Dutch-looking crew. One of the jollyboats brought extra visitors. They were Gold, Twitch, Peg and Patch. The two youngest rats wanted a nose around.

'Nice to be back on our new ship,' said Peg when he saw Rip.

'This is not your ship,' she said with a ratty smile.

'Will you come back now?' said Patch. 'We know how the boat works.'

'With you? No. I have just found my Lu and Preen. I want to stay with them.'

'I will stay too,' said Gold.

'Oh good,' said Rip.

'But what will we do?' said Patch.

'You two are the Skips,' said Rip. 'You know how. You will be great. You know *kree*, you are brave and smart and it's your ship.'

'You can't have two Skips,' said Peg.

'Why would that stop you?' said Rip.

'Hah, you're right,' said Peg. 'Bye Rip.

'Bye Patch. Bye Peg.'

'Bye Rip,' said Patch. 'We will miss you.'

They went back to the jollyboat. Rip would never see them again. She watched the boat float away. In it, she could see the Bigs rescued from the *Amitié*. All of them, men, women and children, smelled a lot healthier and happier than before.

Eventually all the fuss died down. The Dutch-looking crew was ready to go.

'Shall we move the prisoners to the *Liberté*?' Rouge asked Blanche.

'No, there's nowhere safe to put them. They will have to stay here. But we can't let a cargo inspector near the brig.'

Blanche turned to Runa.

'I think it best we change into something a bit prettier before we reach the port of Dejima. Runa, do you have a dress you can wear?'

Runa nodded. There was a pink dress her Pappa bought for her back in the West Indies. She had meant to hem it, but pirating got in the way of needlework, so the bottom of the dress skimmed the floor. It would have to do.

She knew this trip off the ship might be her best chance to get help. Who would believe a messy urchin in trousers too big for her? No one. But they might believe a little lady.

*****

Rip watched Runa sweep past.

She saw something long, pink and swishy and it made her curious. She ran under Runa's skirts.

She found herself in a high tent supported by two skinny legs. The legs started to move. Rip went with them, careful to avoid being squashed by the black patent leather shoes.

Runa walked all the way across the deck and down the gang plank with Rip hidden under her skirts.

'Hello,' she said to Abel who was already at the dock. Rip took the opportunity to escape the skirt and climb up Abel's leg.

'Hullo,' he said.

'She still likes you more than me,' said Runa as Abel picked Rip up and placed her on his shoulder. She liked it there: she had a good view. 'I wish my ratty would do that, but she's too much of a fidget.'

'This one is calm as long as you don't prod her.'

They looked around. Dejima was a very strange place. It was a man-built island joined to the nearest city by a long bridge. The way was shut by gates. The island was curved like a melon slice. It held about forty buildings and a small stand of trees. It was the only place foreign traders were permitted to visit in the whole of Japan.

Runa and the two captains, all disguised as innocent maidens, were the only women in sight.

The pirates were nervous but they hid it well. They left all their weapons on the other ship as they weren't allowed to carry them ashore.

Runa recognised the fake Dutch 'captain' chosen to speak for the crew. It was her old enemy, the second mate, who had clearly taken well to pirate life.

He was talking to the officials as they looked at the paperwork.

At first, it was just Dutchmen who inspected the papers, but soon the Japanese were looking at the forgeries too.

Runa looked at these new men curiously. They all had black hair and were dressed in long, layered silks which swept low to their ankles. Though the outer layers were plain, the inner layers flashed with colour. It was clear they were the ones really in charge. An argument started in two languages.

'What's happening?' whispered Abel, in French.

Runa struggled to make out what was going on. Everyone was speaking very fast.

'They say we should not be here,' said Runa. 'Only two ships a year are allowed to come to Japan and one just left. That would be the one Captain Blanche attacked. The other is still anchored here...'

She stopped.

'What is it?'

'Abel,' she said, slowly. 'Would you like to have a look around?'

'Oh, yes.'

The pair sidled away from the arguing adults.

Rip kept her balance as they walked through Dejima.

Runa and Abel marvelled at the buildings. It was as though a little piece of Europe had lifted up, floated halfway around the world and settled down to root itself on the doorstep of the Silver Empire. They walked to the point nearest the mainland and squinted at the shore. Rip sniffed deeply. Everything smelled new and full of different flavours. She could smell boiling rice, salty soy and frying oil. There was agarwood incense and fish served in sweet, dark sauces. Even the tiles and walls had a different scent.

They had not yet come to the other Dutch ship when Captain Blanche appeared. She moved fast, but uncomfortably, her dress rustling around her.

'Runa, come with me. Come quick, back to the *Liberté*. One of the Dutch officials told us no women are allowed here. We have to go back to the ship now, before we are seen by the Japanese inspector.'

The children were hustled back through the narrow streets and up the gangplank.

Rip hung on to Abel's shoulder. He leaned on a railing and looked back at the island. The pirates and the

Dejima Dutch were already unloading the cargo – the pirates lifting the boxes nearest the brig. Others were taking down and folding up the sails. The Japanese officials demanded they gave them up until all the goods were safely on dry land.

'I can see the masts of the other ship from here,' said Runa, who pushed her long hair under a hat and changed back into her rough-and-ready shirt and trousers.

Rip decided to relax and clean her belly.

Abel looked around and spoke in a low voice.

'You're thinking about telling them about us, aren't you?'

'I have to,' Runa said in a whisper. 'My old captain was good to me. I can't just leave him down there.'

'We've been good to you too,' said Abel.

'You have,' said Runa. She squirmed. 'But it's not right.'

'We will be caught if you let them go.'

'I don't want you hurt,' said Runa. 'I'm trying to find a way to make sure you aren't arrested or hanged.'

'Runa, they will never take us,' said Abel. 'Captain Blanche, Captain Rouge, all the men – and me. We would rather die than be captured.'

'I'd get Pappa to see there was a fair trial,' said Runa, her lip trembling.

'There wouldn't be a trial,' said Abel.

'What do you mean?' said Runa.

'We were slaves, but we escaped. If they catch us, we will be slaves again. And the men will fight until their last drop of blood before they give up their freedom. Some of us already have. Do you understand now?'

Runa was thunderstruck. Suddenly a lot of things she'd missed made sense.

Rip pricked up her ears. She watched the Bigs carefully. Abel was breathing fast. His lip was quivering. Runa had wet eyes.

'I knew some of you, but...'

'All of us. Me too. Blanche led us out of Haiti. There was fire, smoke, blood and battle. Some people fought. But when the smoke cleared it was more of the same. We chose to flee. We'd seen enough fighting.

'We weren't really pirates, not to begin with. We've never really plundered and pillaged. Yours was the first ship we took. We just want to find a place to settle and live free in peace.'

'I had no idea,' she said.

'I won't go back to being owned,' said Abel, his face ashy. 'I have a voice. I want to use it. And that's why I say no. I won't do anything that could get us caught.'

Runa said: 'I would help you, you know, if the tables were turned.'

'Then help me by letting us get away. Promise me.'

'I can't, Abel. You're right. But the old crew need help. I don't know what to do.'

'Please promise.'

'I can't!'

Runa turned. Abel and Rip watched her stamp back to the ship.

# Chapter 17: Rat to the Rescue

It was early the next day. Rip sat on Abel's shoulder as the boy hunkered out of the way. Shifting cargo was difficult, dangerous work, and he had a heavy heart. Runa was his best friend. It felt horrible to fight with her.

Suddenly, Rip stood up and sniff-sniffed. She could smell Runa. The girl Big waited until the men were busy with a heavy bale of tobacco. Then she slipped down the gangplank and onto the island.

'I saw her too, Rat,' said Abel. He hurried after Runa and almost knocked into a brawny pirate dragging a crate by a long hook.

Rip hung on tight. The young Big jogged fast. The ground was a blur. She buried her claws in his shirt and wrapped her tail around the back of his neck.

Runa turned the corner. Abel broke into a sprint to catch her. She heard him and glanced over her shoulder. When she saw them, she ran.

Abel chased Runa past half-a-dozen buildings, his passenger hanging on grimly, before he caught the girl.

'Let go!' she said fiercely when his hand clamped down on her arm.

'No,' said Abel. 'I won't let you do it.'

Rip clung desperately as the two young Bigs fought, pushing and shoving each other. She burrowed into

Abel's shirt for safety. Runa broke free, snatching her arm loose. She tensed to run, but Abel surprised her.

'I know you are trying to do the right thing,' he said.

'I know you are, too,' said Runa. 'I just don't know how we can both be right.' She was still angry but she brushed at her rumpled sleeve.

'I have an idea,' said Abel. 'Your sailors can have their ship back and my pirates can stay free.'

'How?'

'The Dutch head man will be here soon,' said Abel. 'You can tell him about the prisoners on the *Black Caesar*. They will have to sail out to save them. In the meantime we can get a message out to the pirates first. That will give them a chance to get away.'

'How?' said Runa. Then her eyes went round. 'Oh, I know.' She fumbled in her pocket for the paper and pen. 'I knew this would be useful. I can write a message on this for Captain Blanche. But even if this works, that means I'll never see you again. You'll be on the run all your life.'

Abel nodded.

'I'd rather that than be caught.'

'But one day you might be,' said Runa. 'Unless - unless it's you who tells the Dutch men what happened, with me. I'll say you rescued me. My old captain believes me. If you stay here, with no papers, they won't know who you are. They'll only know you are a hero who saved the crew of the *Hydromyst*.'

'But then the *Liberté* will sail without me.'

The children looked at each other, both torn. Abel was in anguish. He stood there, his hands in fists, his shoulders knotted.

'If you come with me,' said Runa, 'you will be able to plot your own course. You can follow your song.'

Abel trembled. Then he became still.

'Right,' he said. 'We will both go. Let's get the note back to the ship. We need another messenger.'

He leaned down to find Rip.

The next thing Rip knew, a hand was around her middle and she was pulled out of the warmth of Abel's shirt.

The children had a devil of a job holding her still. Abel clasped her tight while Runa scribbled a note in French then tried to tie it round the rat's neck. Rip hated this. She whipped herself back and forth like an angry snake. They tried to use leather laces to hold the note fast. Rip thought they felt horrible. She did not like being held still or being bound up. Four times she slipped free and four times she was recaptured.

Abel swore.

'I'm trying,' said Runa.

'I'm sorry, Rat,' said Abel. He grabbed Rip as she managed to slip loose again. 'Please don't hate us. This is a matter of life or death.'

Rip felt a hot, sharp-red urge to bite the gripping hands. She fought it down.

'Not this time. I will not bite you, Bigs,' she squeaked. But she still struggled to get free.

Finally, Runa managed to make a kind of harness and knotted the note into it. Then Abel lowered Rip to the flagstones.

'I hope she makes it back to the ship,' he said.

'I'm sure she'll run straight there,' said Runa. 'It's where she feels safe.'

This was a bad experience for Rip, especially when she took one look around and realised she was in a strange place. Her ordeal had only just begun. She tugged on Abel's trouser leg, hoping to be picked up again. He gently moved her away with his foot.

'Go,' he said.

The Bigs were the only familiar things she could sense. Despite feeling outraged at her treatment, she stood on her back legs and stretched up to Abel, but he shooed her away.

'Go on home!' he said. Then he and Runa set off to find the Customs Office.

Rip did not like being shouted at. She ran to a wall and pressed against it, slinking with her belly to the ground.

'Nooo,' said Runa. 'She's going the wrong way.' But Rip paid no notice.

Everything was very bright. It was the middle of the day and the sun was hot. She was confused. She could smell seawater in every direction. In one house she could hear water bubbling as it boiled, ready for noodles and broth. In the other, someone was playing a stringed instrument. There were Bigs clanking and banging as they worked in warehouses. A white cat lounged on a roof, lazily soaking up the sun. It twitched an ear as Rip's claws clattered on stone.

Rip felt abandoned, angry and frightened. She wanted to be back on the ship she knew so well. The rat had no idea how important the paper on her back was but it annoyed her. She tried to bite it but it moved. The leather laces strained against her front legs.

It isn't often the fates of dozens of people are decided by one little animal. Rip could have slipped into a crevice or climbed up one of the buildings into the attic and lived out her life in Japan. But she wanted to go home.

Rip scurried.

Dejima was a small island; a human could cross in minutes. But to Rip, who was just six inches long from her nose to her bottom, and who was used to life on a ship, this was a dangerous and epic journey.

She crept around the side of a barrel and sniffed, trying to find a scent-trail that would lead her home.

There it was!

She darted forward then froze. Something was wrong.

Then the sky went dark as the fat cat sitting on the roof jumped and flew down at her like an assassin.

# Chapter 18: Rip on the Run

Rip felt the cat's presence before he landed. She went from still to full speed in an instant. This saved her life. If the cat landed on Rip her back would have snapped.
  The cat took a moment to shake himself. The landing rattled his bones. Then he looked up, the pupils in his eyes narrowed to mad black needles.

Rip moved as quick as a flash, zooming across an alleyway and into a narrow gutter.

The cat sniffed her out. He found her sliding through a gap between the stones. She felt his hot breath on her fur.

Rip had never encountered a cat before, but she remembered the nightmare stories she'd heard as a tiny ritten. Her mother warned all her brothers and sisters about Cats with a capital C. It stood for for cruelty, claws and craftiness. A cat had eaten Rip's father. She trembled. This was not a danger she could plan for.

A huge paw fished down the gutter, four curved blades extended from it, all pin sharp. The cat was trying to scoop her out of the gap.

Rip sped up, following the line of the drain. The cat followed, his triangle nose pushing between the stones. He snapped and bit with teeth as long as Rip's forearms. His breath stank of rancid meat.

A paw smashed down behind Rip. It withdrew. She ran helter-skelter forward until a second paw blocked her way.

She sprang straight up like a flea.

The cat's jaw snapped shut on thin air.

Rip reached the top of her leap and tumbled back down. She landed on fur and instinctively gripped tight.

She was on the cat's back, between his shoulders.

The cat was baffled for a moment. Then he realised where Rip was.

He twisted about, yowling with rage. Rip clung on, knowing her life depended on it. She was riding a tiger.

This cat swivelled and wriggled, trying to seize Rip. When that didn't work, he bucked like a bronco. Rip felt her claws loosen, even though they were buried in the cat's scruff. At the last moment she let go and kicked, using the cat's motion to push herself through the air.

She flew, her feet stretched out. Her fingers and toes hit the wooden frame of a Japanese house. She hugged it like a sticky burr.

The cat squatted below, his tail swishing. He hissed, showing a very pink throat.

Rip swarmed up the wooden post in a series of jumps, her hands and feet clamping in turn as she went up.

The cat circled on the ground below before slinking away.

Rip reached the top. She ran along the middle of the steep roof, her claws clicking on the shingles. She held herself low in case a bird swooped down to grab her.

The roof covered several houses. Rip hurried to the edge and slid down from the peak of the roof, but she lost her footing. The shingles at the edge curved up and she was catapulted over the side and landed on top of a gateway arch.

She hadn't lost the cat. He saw Rip the same moment Rip smelled him.

She made a blind, panicked leap. It took her to a window covered by a paper screen. The screen swung out of the way and she fell onto a woven grass floor mat. Rip shot under the first thing she saw, which happened to be a bamboo table.

Two Dutch men in dark blue waistcoats were sitting at the table while a pretty but solemn-looking young woman served them fragrant tea. Her face was painted in white and red, she had artfully blackened teeth and long silk sleeves draped from her arms. She made a little noise when she saw Rip but did not spill the tea. Then the cat smashed through the window, the two men leaped to their feet and the delicate teapot went flying.

The cat dived under the table. Rip zipped beneath the silken skirts of the woman who screamed when she felt the rat's soft, warm fur against her sandaled feet.

One of the men shooed the cat out. The other went to console the woman and Rip took the chance to hurry out of the back door.

The dazed rat blinked in the daylight. She had no idea which way to go, so she shuffled along the side of a warehouse, sniff-snuffing every inch of the way. Her little heart bounced against her ribs. She stopped to have a good scratch and clear her head.

An almighty sound filled her ears.

'*Nezumi*!' roared a Big. He came running at her holding a long stick with a thick bushy end. Rip held herself still, hoping that he would lose sight of her, but that didn't work for Bigs. The enormous stick came down like a falling tree. Rip braced herself to become a splat on the doorstep.

She was pressed down by dozens of strands of straw which parted around her. She'd been hit by the bristle end of the brush and it hadn't hurt her one bit,

She swore at the Big.

'PEEP!'

And then she was off and running again, the rolled note bouncing up and down on her back.

When she got to a crossroads, a dog barked at her furiously and Bigs shouted in disgust. Though rats were common in ports across the globe, they seldom went jogging down a street in broad daylight.

Rip ran non-stop, further than she'd ever run before. She stopped trying to use her nose, which was confused by all the new smells. Instead, she used her ears. She strained. A faint song came to her. The sailors on her ship were singing shanties as they hauled the cargo. There! She chirped and turned to the sound.

There was a little copse of trees near where the *Black Caesar* was moored. Rip reached this shelter and paused beneath a wide, waxy-green leaf. Her legs were aching and shaking but she could smell the unique cocktail of sweaty men, rat markings, salt-crusted wood and dried herbs and furs that marked her ship. It smelled good to her.

There was only a short dash left and she would be safe on board.

Then she heard a strange clicking noise. She went still, freezing every muscle from her nose to her tail, but she strained to look as far left as her eyes would allow.

It was the moon-faced cat. He had his head low, his rump was in the air and he was ready to pounce.

# Chapter 19: The Crew and their Captain

Many of the rats on the *Black Caesar* were napping, but some were about on business. Those scavenging nearest the dock stopped and lifted their heads. They could hear shrill squeaking, angry and afraid. Pink ears pricked up. A dozen rats scrambled to get a view of the commotion. Sleek, Thug and Preen were among them. Lu joined their group.

'What is it?' said the little white rat. She squinted to see; her ruby-red eyes were poorer than everyone else's.

'It's Rip!' said Sleek.

'Rip?' said Gold, popping out of a bucket. 'Where?'

'Down there,' said Sleek.

'I smell a beast on the hunt,' said Thug, nervously. The little dot that was Rip came closer. There was a bigger shape behind her and it was catching up in swift bounds.

'Oh no,' Preen twittered. 'Oh no, oh no!'

'Run, Rip, run,' squeaked Lu.

Rip was already running. She was tired. Rats do short sprints, not marathons. Her limbs went as fast as they could but they were getting tangled in the leather laces. The note unravelled and flapped loose like a parachute. It slowed her down. The cat closed the gap.

'What can we do?' wailed Preen.

There was nothing they could do.

Rip reached the bottom of the gangplank. One of the loops holding the paper in place caught around her back leg and she stumbled. The cat pounced.

'Ee!' said Lu.

'No!' said Preen.

There was a dreadful squeal. All the rats flinched. When they dared to look, the cat was still there. He was hunched over.

Rip was not in his mouth. She was not under his paw.

The cat had pounced but she pounced back and bit hard on his foot. She danced around in front of him, hissing. The cat growled back and took a swipe with its other paw.

'Rip bit the cat,' said Preen in wonder.

'No cats can board our ship,' said Sleek. 'It can't come up here.'

'Get the cat!' said Gold.

'Let's help Rip,' said Lu.

'Chase it off!' said Twitch.

Suddenly everyone was running at the tom cat. A dozen fighting-fit pi-rats were all puffed up and ready to protect their ship.

The cat's eyes turned to saucers. His tail puffed like a feather duster. This meal was far too much trouble. He decided to leave. The rats ran the cat from the dock, chittering and cheering.

'Yes, get lost, cat,' called Lu.

The tom cat retreated to a safe distance. Then he sat down, lifted his leg to wash his bottom, and pretended the whole sorry business never happened.

Rip was surrounded by friendly noses. She was patted with gentle paws and sniff-sniffed over and over until she was giddy.

'Thank you,' she said. 'Thank you all,'

But all of a sudden, her friends fell away. She felt a hand grasp her and her feet left the deck. The Bigs noticed the cat fight.

'This one has a note on its back,' said one of the pirates. 'I'll hand it to the cap'n, double-quick.'

He let Rip go and hurried off.

She was grateful to shake off the laces and feel free again. She left the bindings in a pile on the deck. The rats barely had time to find hidey-places when, suddenly, the bell rang.

The Bigs were everywhere, hurriedly filling the jollyboats with best goods. Both boats were full of men. Captain Blanche carried a bag of gold in one hand and her neck and arms dripped with jewellery. Other pirates hastily loaded up on everything they could carry by hand. Once the row boats launched, they heaved and ho'ed at the oars. In less than half an hour, the ship was deserted and the pirates and the rescued slaves were well on their way back to the hidden *Liberté*.

By the time the Dutch officials arrived with a dozen armed men, it was far too late. The pirates were nowhere to be seen. Nor could the Dutch give chase because the Japanese had taken their sails.

Captain Blanche and her crew escaped.

\*\*\*\*\*

Much later, once the imprisoned sailors were freed and led blinking into the sunlight, and well after the words *Black Caesar* were scrubbed from the ship's name plate, Runa and Abel sat at very front of the ship feeding scraps to their three favourite rats.

'Do you think they made it?' said Abel, looking out to sea.

'I know they did,' said Runa.

'Rat really saved the day, didn't she?' said Abel, feeding Rip a noodle. 'And she'll never even really understand how.'

'Everyone thinks you saved me, and I rescued my old crew. They don't know you actually saved the pirates too. But none of that really matters.'

'I hope they remember me,' said Abel.

'They will. Abel, the boy who gave them freedom.'

Abel laughed.

Rip, meanwhile, was happy simply to tussle with her sisters and feast until her belly stretched. Her battle with the cat was already legend among the ship rats. Life seemed good.

'Where do you think we will go next?' said Lu as the Bigs fixed the sails back in place.

'I don't know,' said Rip.

Lu said, 'I'm glad to sail with you once more.'

'Yes,' said Preen. 'We three will sail on.'

'And we will find home,' said Rip.

The end, for now…

# Glossaries

**Ship terms**:

**Barque**: A small ship, often used for trading. Favoured by pirates due to its speed and because it could be sailed by a small crew.

**Basket**: A lookout place at the top of the mast. Used before crow's-nests became common.

**Fore**: The front of the ship

**Fluyt**: a big cargo ship used very successfully by the Dutch from the 1500s. The Fluyt in this story was built in the late 1700s

**Hold**: Where cargo, food and tools are kept

**Hull**: The "skin" of the ship. Keeps air in and water out (hopefully)

**Orlop**: The deck where ropes are stored

**Port**: On the left, if you are facing forward on a ship

**Prow**: The very front of the ship, the part that pushes through the sea

**Scuppers**: A gap to allow water to drain from the deck. Rats use them as windows

**Stem**: The foremost part of the ship, an extension of the keel. Like a mast that sticks out forward

**Starboard**: On the right, if you are facing forward on a ship

Rat terms:

**A Mischief**: The term for a gang of rats, like a flock of birds or pack of dogs

**Bigs**: Gigantic two-legged creatures regarded as slow but dangerous. They are messy and leave food around. Otherwise known as "humans"

**Brux/Bruxing**: This is when a rat grinds their top and bottom teeth together. It can be a sign of nerves but also of happiness

**Buck**: A male rat

**Doe**: A female rat

**Kree**: The rat word for the code they live by to keep peace

**Ritten**: A baby rat. Used sometimes instead of the "true" term kitten to avoid them getting mixed up with baby cats

**Skip**: The leader of the ship rats, the equivalent of a human captain or "skipper"

**Sniff-sniff**: A polite greeting. Sniffing allows one rat to find out who the other rat is and what they have been up to

# Endnote

Real-life rats have a poor reputation across the world. But did you know there are actual hero rats out there today?

In fact, an organisation called APOPO trains African giant pouched rats (nicknamed HeroRATs!) to sniff out a very infectious disease to help stop its spread.

Although they are only very distantly related to brown (Norwegian) rats like Lu, Preen and Rip, African giant pouched rats are just as curious and clever. They are cheap to train, have an excellent sense of smell and learn to get along very well with their human handlers.

HeroRATs have learned to detect Tuberculosis, which allows medics in isolated parts of the world to test patients on the spot.

Before the HeroRATs came along, doctors had to send people home and wait for the results to come back. That meant more people could catch the illness and get sick.

Now, thanks to some clever ratty noses, doctors can treat ill people right away, which could save many lives.

This book has been released to support the work of APOPO and its HeroRATs. Please consider adopting a HeroRAT, donating to the organisation or letting other people know about this book and the work APOPO rats do.

To find out more visit www.support.apopo.org

This book was written on a not-for-profit basis. Approximately 50p from each sale will go to APOPO. The rest of the recommended retail price cover the costs of printing and distribution. Amounts may vary according to the publishing format you have chosen to purchase.

You can find out more about the author on www.facebook.com/RhiWaller or follow Lu on Twitter at @LuSniffy.

The author has no official links to APOPO. Thank you for reading this story.

# About the author

Rhian Waller was born in Lincolnshire, grew up in North Wales and is a lecturer and occasional freelance journalist in Chester.

She is interested in almost everything and enjoys writing, reading, martial arts, bush craft training, travel, live music, hill walking, SCUBA diving and gaming.

She loves getting reviews most of all. They are like tips for authors. Please leave one on Amazon or Goodreads.

Leeloo, Priss and Ripley, the rats who inspired this book, were adopted from the RSPCA and live in Chester. They like sunflower seeds and snoozing in hammocks.

Watch out for Spy Rats: A Tale of Secrets on the High Seas. The final book in the *Rat Tales Trilogy* will be out soon.

And introducing...

A book about poetry and friendship for younger readers. Also coming soon.

9 780244 386504